SPARKY'S TREASURE

WARNING THIS BOOK CONTAINS REFERENCES WHICH CAN CAUSE STRESS AND TRIGGERS.

THIS IS FOR 18 YEAR OLDS AND OVER.

*Yasmin
Lovely to meet you!
Hugs
X Spencer X*

COPYRIGHT

Copyright © 2018 By K. Spencer

All rights reserved. This book or any portion thereof

may not be reproduced or used in any manner whatsoever

without the express written permission of the publisher

except for the use of brief quotations in a book review.

The names, companies, references are purely coincidental as this is a book of fiction. And has came from the authors imagination.

For more information or to request permission contact: kirstyh2447@gmail.com

ACKNOWLEGMENT

Well what can I say? This is my hardest book to write so far. As always thank you to my Daddy who always said do what makes you happy.

Thank you to my family. Especially my son and daughter who were constantly telling me, I'm the best ever. My husband who put up with the constant click click click of the keyboard. As well as taking over the computer.

To my sister Dawn who helped with the name Bobo.

My bestie James who is always telling me that he is proud, although not as proud as I am of him.

My Betas who kick some serious ass by helping me better myself. Thank you ladies.

And massive huge thank you to both my Photographer and cover photo editor, Kate you are bloody awesome.

And my gorgeous model Katrina, you gave me exactly what I wanted, you're awesome of awesomeness.

CHAPTER ONE

SPARKY

I can't get this out of my head. That one word, that has destroyed my fucking world. NO. NO. NO. It's like it's on repeat over and over and over again. She was, and if I'm honest still is my world. But that kid of hers would have been conceived around the same time she left.

No I'm not going to think on it any more. I'm going to get blind drunk and find a dirty whore to fuck until I pass out.

Just as I go to the bar I see who is serving and sneer at her. Why the fucking hell is she here still. She doesn't need the money, so she must like fucking with my head; well no fucking more she doesn't.

"If it isn't the whore with money."

"Step off Sparky, you don't want my men to put a bullet in your left ass cheek do you? You piss me off and I will happily allow Seb to come in here and shoot your backside for being a grade A bitch to me."

"Always having to have a shooter, what can't do shit on your own Treas.. bitch!" I snap out.

Yes I know I'm a giant a-hole but she is a fucking bitch who must have slept with someone else while with me.

Her phone rings and she takes a step back to answer it "Hey what's wrong?" pause "Ok I will be there in a minute, take his temp and I will get him to urgent care."

She grabs her purse and goes to walk out of the bar when I stop her and say "What's wrong with little man?"

"None of your business Sparky. Now step away from me."

"No tell me, please. I'm fed up of being left out of shit involving you. You are my fucking wife, I have a right to know what the fuck is going on!"

I shouldn't have shouted that out. No one knew we got married in Vegas. I promised her no one would know.

Just as I go to apologize I feel my balls hit my mouth fast.

Yep I fucking knew I should have kept my mouth shut.

"Where were you the night I was being raped oh husband of mine? That's right cock deep in Melissa's snatch. Stay away from me and my son" and she walks out.

"You did what?" Princess roars from across the room and I know just by the way she shouted that shit that not only am I in fucking agony from my nuts but that if it wasn't for my Pres I would be getting the shit kicked out of me by the one and only Princess.

Coughing I groan out "Not now Princess please"

Getting up off the ground I message Millie and ask her to come take care of my balls. Fucking women and going for the nuts what is with that shit!

I need to sort this shit with Jessie. If she had told me what had happened all those years ago, I would have sorted it there and then. But she was the one who stepped away from me, she never once said that me fucking other women bothered her. Surely she would have fucking said, which means she is using that shit against me. Well fuck her. Its time she stepped the fuck away again. She can stay away from me far a fucking way.

Millie appears at the doors to the kitchen and gives me her 'I want your dick' smile. Yeah she can wait until she has taken care of the pain in my cock. Fucking bitches just think of no one but themselves, well fuck that. No more being taken for a god damn pussy whipped bitch.

Turning to the back door I stride to it with my fucking head held high. I slam out the door knowing every one of my brothers are watching me and no doubt thinking I'm allowing a woman to hurt me like that. We all respect women we never harm them but my god am I close to having her hide. She will learn shortly that I don't allow anyone to disrespect me in my own goddamned club.

I get on my Dyna Glide and start her up. She has been named Treasure. I bought her not two weeks after my Jessie left named her after my ol lady she may have left but Treasure is and always will be my reminder of Jessie. I may have not had Jessie long but she was mine, technically still is. I never divorced her and I never denounced her as my ol lady, as far as the club knows she is still my ol lady. I don't think I could have ever denounced her but hearing that she kept the child she conceived from a rape has me thinking what the fuck she was thinking, my cousin couldn't even carry one to term after she was raped.

Yet here is my treasure who not only kept the child but isn't afraid to say he is the product of a rape! I'm in two minds do I ignore that fact that she is raising a baby from a rape or do I applaud her for having the strength to admit it freely?

I head out of the club and turn left and just drive aimlessly around for a few hours, I head back towards town and home when I spot her car outside of the hospital. Our tiny town doesn't have a lot but the one thing it does have is an all-night doctors surgery ran by one of the brothers family. They got fed up with people phoning at all hours so set this up.

Pulling up beside her car, I begin to think this is one of the most stupidest ideas I've ever had. Getting off my treasure I head towards the double doors to the hospital and I can see two of her guys looking like they want my head on a fucking stick and my body roasted for their diners.

"Yo what's wrong with little man." I ask Seb.

He drags his eyes over me like I am the biggest pile of cow shit that he has ever seen yet answers me with a short "Nothing with you"

Chuckling I walk past him and head directly to the room Jessie is in with little man. Passing one of the women at the reception she leers at me. Yeah I ain't fucking this one up. Here comes Sparky, Treasure you ain't ready for what's coming.

Opening the door I see her with him in her arms singing some song that is most definitely not familiar to me which must mean it's one of her music. Seriously she can't teach the kid some country or some good old rock? No of course not has to be hardcore. Saying that he is looking calm not compared to every other kid I've seen in a hospital.

Looking at her without her noticing I'm here. I'm amazed at how much she has, but also, hasn't changed. She has put a little bit of weight on but that's a bloody good thing as she was always way too skinny. Her hair is no longer the light brown it's now more like a fucking unicorn decided to decorate her head with every color in the rainbow. Saying that, it's strangely fucking sexy. Just thinking of her spread out with her hands tied to the bottom posts of our bed with her head slightly over the edge of the bed and one foot tied to the swing above our bed and the other wrapped around my head as I taste the sweet pussy. Ok, ok change that thought can't speak to her with the hard-on from hell on, she will never want me near her even if I am the best she will ever have.

"Treasure what is wrong with little man? Let me help at least." Praying she will turn and talk to me. She just lifts her head and gives me a look of pure hate.

"If my son wasn't ill right now I would happily say what needs to be said, but as he is currently ill and in the fricking hospital I am just going to say go on home Sparky. I ain't in the mood or got the energy to deal with you on top of everything else that happens to be currently going on." She said as if she wasn't even talking to me but a fucking stranger.

Didn't expect that, she has always been a fire cracker. It must be because the kid. "Look I just want to help. Even if it's something as mundane as getting a coffee or getting you a tissue. Let someone help Jessie."

"Huh, pretty sure I have Seb, Ton and even Gregor to help. I don't need nor do I want you to help with my son. He is fine just needs his mum not a complete stranger. If you do not leave I will make sure you leave and I certainly won't use my men to do it. That fun part is all for me once I get my son down for a nap which, Sparky boy, you are fu..mucking up by being here and interrupting his song kindly leave."

My jaw drops well fuckkkk me. She still has her fire. Well guess I stand outside then and wait for her royal fucking highness to leave the room. To her I nod and leave with the parting "See you in a bit my Treasure" seeing her stiffen brings a smile to my face. Bring it on Jess bring it the fuck on.

CHAPTER 2

JESSIE

That son of a bitch. No I can't call him a son of a bitch, his mum is nice. The fucking assmunching fucknut of a wankstain. I won't swear in front of my baby boy, I won't. Its bloody hard not to though.

Here I am in the hospital because he has had an allergic reaction to nuts. I fucking told his nanny no nuts no nuts noooooo nuts. Not give him a fucking peanut butter sandwich. Safe to say her ass is well and truly fired and if it wasn't for the fact I was in a frigging hospital she would be ten feet under by now. But alas I need to be nice and keep calm although I certainly don't feel calm. Then to top my shit cake of a day off asshole brain just had to come to the hospital to be all sweet and nice.

Yeah, no that isn't going to happen I can't deal with that and everything else. After what happened between us and my rape I just can't go back. Sparky ain't the man for me, he was my mistake in life. Ok he wasn't a bad mistake just not the mistake I wished he was.

I understand him being pissed I ran away. But after seeing him with that slut bag, that broke my heart, but then to be raped but his so called brother the same day I just couldn't face him and I didn't want him being hurt and ashamed every time he looked at me if he found out. The only man I have even remotely thought of since that horrible day has been Seb and that was only because we spar and he gets me hotter than hell that first time I got turned on freaked me the fuck out.

6 MONTHS AGO

I had way too much energy to spare. My baby boy was with my nana and she had told me, and not in a nice way, to go away and have me time. I didn't have a clue what to do so I went to my fathers' friends' sons gym. Long way around that is to say the guy who looks like he is a tank with a colorful fucking rainbow of ink. Ok not that bad but when he has a phoenix, a tiger and several evil looking guns and skulls and "I am gods punishment" tattooed on his upper chest he doesn't give me the smiles I was hoping for when I look at him. Although bonus he is gruff and fucking yummier than any man I have seen. I may not be able to fuck him but at least I have eye candy while I exercise.

"Who are you and why are you in my gym?" I swear I feel like I'm about to jump clean out my skin but father taught me better than that. I look down at my nails as if he is purely here for me to wait on. I slowly lift my head looking first at his thighs in his shorts, oh my, are they toned. Muscle upon muscle then as I skim my eyes past what looks like a very, very impressive bulge in his black shorts which really need to be slightly tighter as I can't get a full look at that dick print. Then up again I see he is wearing a t-shirt which is just a crime against nature. White t-shirt with the black and blue writing that states its "Lions Gym"

As I get to his face, that is all heavy lines and looks like he has been attacked by a glass bottle years before, I see he has a scowl on his face.

"Do I need to repeat?" he grits out as though it's a fucking damn chore to talk to me. What the hell??

"One, don't talk to me like I'm insignificant and two, I'm here to blow off energy and I am no one you need to know other than someone who requires the fucking use of your gym. If I can't use it all you had to say was sorry but it's exclusive." I say aloud yet think what a fucking wanker you are asshole.

"You are someone who shouldn't be in my gym never mind blowing of some energy. Go home little girl. Go and get daddy or husband to blow off energy with." He sneers at me as though I really am shit on his shoe.

Oh fuck no he didn't. "Tell you what. Make a deal? If I can get you knocked out with four hits you let me work out here for however long I'm here. If I fail I will stay the fuck away and never darken your door again."

He is looking directly in my eyes and its giving me the heebie jeebies there's no other words although pissing my panties scared may also work.

"Deal! Come"

"I am not a fucking dog asshole, treat me with the respect I deserve." I ground out through my teeth.

"No but you are a bitch." He rolls his eyes at me.

Who the hell is this moron. Ah fuck it he is about to fingers crossed hit the deck. "Shall we?" I ask as I step into the ring. With a slight nod from him I wait for him to take stance. When he doesn't I'm confused. Tilting his head he looks as though he is bored.

"Bitches first" at that I take a step forward and take my own stance and smile a sweet smile "Well you might want to go since you are about to become my bitch"

His face twitches as though he has seen something seriously nasty. This will be fun.

He throws his left, I dodge narrowly missing the fist and as I do I throw a right to his jaw and connect. He shakes his head and throws another left as I avoid the left he curves a right into my ribs. Son of a bitch! That stung. Fuck this. One hit asshole! Is all I think as I hit him with my left upper cut hit his chin and firmly plant a right just to sweeten the pot as he hit the floor with an almighty bang. Fucking asshole hit the ribs that literally just healed after being broken from my fathers' enforcer during training.

Men, and hitting the ribs. Seriously! I get out the ring and look at my fathers' friend whom is standing with a smile a mile wide. "When he wakes up tell him to add my name to the list. Fucking asshole, hope he feels like utter fucking shit"

Going home all I can think is tomorrow will be fun.

Next day I get kicked out the house and head to the gym. Seb is standing there with a smile and says "Sorry I didn't know who you were and you walked in like sex on legs. Spar me a bit?"

While sparring with him he kept trying to stay clear of my left. He also liked to stare into my eyes and smile. Walking out of that ring I was horny as fuck all I could imagine was sparring with him in the bed or on the mat or on his desk.

I need sex. No I need something better than sex I need fucked hard! I need someone to toss me around a bed and pound my pussy till she is fucking sore. Safe to say I went to a shop and bought a new vibrator.

Every day since then Seb has been in my sex filled dreams.

Then shit hit the fan and my father died. Although died wasn't the word more like desecrated demolished and murdered. Then being told that I am now the head of the family, that never scared me more than being asked by Princess to come home.

CHAPTER 3

SPARKY

I can't understand why I'm currently in a bed that isn't my own. How drunk was I? I turn to get out of the bed that definitely is not mine yet reminds me of someone. Getting up I hold on to the wall for support. My head feels like a battering ram hit it with an anvil and a bull at the same time. I hit the stereo on and all I hear is a lullaby tune, somewhere over the rainbow. Whose fucking room is this a 6 year olds, what the fuck.. nope I know whose room this is. Fuck me save my head. Its Treasures room none other than The Prophet & Brennan Heart - Wake Up! is currently blaring through the speakers. Just as I'm about to try and turn it off, as of course she has it rigged to the whole clubhouse so she can listen while cleaning.

Phantom comes through the door like hell on earth. "Fucking shit head wakes me up with this one every morning. Fucking little shit. Woah why are you in

Jessie's' room Spark? Where is little man? He usually turns this on to wake me for breakfast."

I'm too busy trying to get my head around the fact he just walks straight in my wife's' room like it's a daily thing. "Fuck head she is in the hospital with wee man. What the hell are you doing just walking in? She could have been naked."

He smirks and says "She usually sneaks into Sebs' room down the hall around 3 am dumb ass. How long have you been here with her now?"

Shaking my head I shout "Get to fuck. She won't be going to Seb anymore. Fucking watch this space no more just walking in, I will deal with her and our her son from now on."

Fucking Seb! Can I kill this fucker yet? Oh wait, no as she and he are 'In business together'. Whatever the fuck that shit means.

Turning I walk to the shower and spot a pile of papers that are from a bank and a gym. Looking through them I spot a letter from her father I'm guessing, I can't help but read it.

Dear My Jess

If you have received this it means that you have been handed the reigns to the famiglia, I cannot apologise enough that I won't be there to help you through this change and help guide you. Just know that Seb and the guys will always be there. The one thing to remember is protect family and they will always protect you. I may not have protected you from that filth from the club and what he done to you but remember that you will be granted your revenge. And revenge you shall have. All info has been sent with Seb about that filth who dared to touch my perfect little girl. Remember that you know your training. Teach that grandson of mine that he shall never be allowed to taint our family. Teach him all about the family and who we are. How we will always conquer our foes and that we are the famiglia and no one will stop our family from ruling with an iron fist.

Daughter of mine there is a sister out there that I cannot say for sure exactly where but last I heard she was with a member of the club or a members' sister, not full blood. Find her and when you do find her mother and kill the bitch. She dared to try to kill not only me but your mother, she succeeded in killing your uncle before she flew for the states. This is the only task I ask. I know this is not what you thought the letter would ask. I need this so I can punish her for her crimes against the famiglia .

I have left instructions with the guys.

I love my little girl I wish I never had to write this letter but in the business we are in it is needed. I have not been the best father in the world but I will also say I'm not the worst. I know there is someone after me. And there are only two people in the world who know who. One is in the states and the other is my killer who no doubt will head to the states to kill her.

Find your mother my babushka find her and bring the famiglia back together.

Love papa

What the fuck?

CHAPTER 4

SOFIA

I read the letter that has just dropped through my letter box. The tears flowing have me getting up and turning to the kitchen where the one man who will know what to do. My guard, for 7 years I have been hidden away. Feeling like I should be doing something, helping my husband, my daughter something anything other than being kept safe. What was the point in me being safe if I couldn't save my famiglia.

"It's time to go Marko I can't be without my daughter, my husband has been killed and I want everyone on this. You were his best friend it is time to do something other than sitting in this house living a lie. This is our family time to protect it. Get our shit we are leaving to get my daughter and grandson."

Marko looks hurt and then pissed "We will be on the road within an hour. I know where she is."

I'm a Granma sure she makes me a nana. I don't know how she is going to take it as she was told I had died not 7 years previously, but shit happens and we move on. Let's hope the whore who took my husbands' illegitimate daughter with her after killing her husband is around I want a piece of that bitch.

I walk the length of my hall and stand in front of the room that holds the cameras to my house and garden all is clear so I head up the stairs to pack, walking into my room I see Marko in all his glory. The man may be in his early 50s but oh my lord is he a fine specimen, he has muscles for days a soft grey coming through his hair and his back ripples with the muscles as he moves. You may be thinking I'm such a slut but I have always had two men in my life my husband and my guard. My guard has always been my lover, can't marry two men. Well not legally anyway.

Marko has been my rock when I couldn't have peter he has been there throughout my heart ache of not seeing my daughter grow. If we had a choice I wouldn't have left, I would have fought the devil himself to stay and protect my famiglia but alas, my father was a tyrant and a murderer, sadly so is my brother. I know he killed my husband my peter. And he will try and kill my Jessicka my little hellionesa (I have called her that since she was in my womb). I will be dead and buried before I allow that psycho anywhere near my girl and my grandson.

It's time for the head of my side of the family to take her place. And hell and fire to anyone who dares to stand in my way.

"Mmm my Queen looks like she wants to bathe in the blood of her enemies. You keep that look up and I'm going to bend you over this bed and fuck that ass of yours." Marko smoothly says with that hot look of pure sex.

Huffing out "Don't threaten me with a good time if you aren't willing to put out. Marko how are we going to deal with Jessie? She thinks we are dead. What 'Hi mummy's' girl. We lied I'm alive now let me have my grandson' can see that going down well"

Shaking my head I turn to start packing my clothes in the duffle bag that has stored passports and spare money. As I start stuffing my trousers in the bag I'm lifted and tossed onto the bed.

I scream and know my man is about to do damage to his pussy. I can't call it mine as it's has always been his and Peters.

Marko has a smirk a mile wide on his face "Who the fuck said I wasn't going to put out. I just thought that I would let you have this little power play you think you have continue as its turning me on. But since you asked so nicely I'm going to fuck you hard my Queen. Strip and spread them."

I do as told and slowly start to take my red skull top off all while his eyes follow its movement. His eyes get darker knowing he is about to have me bare before him. No matter how many times he has seen me naked he still looks at me as though it's the first time and he is unwrapping a gift.

"Move baby, I can't wait any longer. Get naked now"

I get naked faster if there was a button that could get rid of all my clothes faster I would as his hungry look spurs me on. As I'm bared to him he smiles and dives his head between my 42E breasts and licks from the left to the right then I feel him swirl his tongue around my nipple then trail it down my ribs along the side of my waist and down my leg to my ankle where he nibbles the ankle and starts licking and nibbling up the inside of my right leg and when he reaches my pussy he blows on it with slow breathes. He slowly licks my clit and then drops to delve his whole tongue into me. I arch off the bed and can't stop the moan that comes out of me he continues to delve his tongue into me and then starts to strum his fingers against my clit and I know I'm done for he knows I'm about to explode as he gets faster then just as I'm about to release he stops and quickly slams his big beast of a cock in me and pounds into me with such precision. He grabs my face and makes me look him in the eyes and ponds home he is rough and knows that I need it harder so harder he does. He keeps eye contact with me and I can feel and see he is about to cum. I am as well and I know he knows as he is gripping my hair and snarls "Fuck that's it my Queen let go." As he says that we both cum hard I bite his shoulder and he applies so much pressure on my hands that I know I'm going to be bruised tomorrow. And I don't give a shit.

"Oh my lord! Marko you are a fuckin god. I love you, but we still need to get on the road." I chuckle.

"Fuck sake give me a minute to kiss you before you de man me. I love you my Queen always will. Now move ass time to go see Jess." He laughs.

Packing everything after a much needed shower for us both. We are on the road heading to Jessicka.

CHAPTER 5

SEB

Hearing a ping while I stand guard outside my sons room, he may not be blood but I have raised that boy so he is my son. I take it out my back pocket and read

Marko: On way. Be ready for fireworks.

Me: Fuck!

Marko: Ha-ha pretty much. See you soon boy.

Me: Amendment Fuck you old man. See you in a few. We are at hospital nothing serious will be home in a few.

Marko: Ok

Shit. Why are they coming? Jess doesn't know her mother is alive nor her Uncle Marko. Very much doubt she knows her uncle Marko is fucking her mother and has been since way before she was born, and I am definitely not telling her that one. I like the sex we have and nothing will stop that, she is my Queen and I'm her King.

I turn on my heel and walk through the doors to Simons' room and wrap my arms around Jessie and she leans her back to my shoulder. Kissing her on the head I ask "How's our little man? Simon needs to come home and we need to talk. Just remember you can't shoot me when we do talk."

I feel her frown. "Are you ending it?" she asks

"Fuck no!"

"Is this talk your fault?"

"Nope it is your parents"

"Daddy died mums dead don't see the problem." She dismisses.

"Well that's not entirely true. Just wait until we get home and get him settled."

"Fine Seb." She is about to say more but the Doctor walks in interrupting us.

"Discharge papers Mrs Marks. Simon is fine. Just make sure you watch what you give him. As a lot of things have nuts in them. There is a script for his epi-pen please fill it in and check with your doctor. I do need to discuss measurement findings with you, it was found that Simons head is small. Smaller than a child of his age. I want your doctor to monitor his heads growth over a period to double check my findings but it would seem your son has something called Microcephaly. Which stands for Small Head but without testings' we shall not know the extent. Which is why I want Simon monitored via your doctor, and I will get in contact with a Paediatrician. As I said it may just be as his head hasn't fully grown yet or it could be he has Microcephaly."

"Doc I would rather know what it could be than not know at all but surely it will be because he is still growing. He is only a baby still."

"That's why I want him measured more. To prove me wrong but he is small headed for his age group."

"Ok doc well I'm going to get little man in the car while my baby girl packs his stuff up." I direct her. One thing at a time. I will read up on this tonight.

As the doctor leaves I spot Sparky waiting in the hall. Shaking my head I tap Jess and nod in his direction as she looks at me. She rolls her eyes and doesn't give me the go ahead to kill this prick.

"How is wee man?" he asks. Fucking hate Simon being called wee man. His name is Simon, use it. Jessie named him Simon not wee man.

"Simon is fine he is going home so if you don't fucking mind Move" I say softly knowing Simon is awake and I refuse to swear around him.

"Are you fucking serious? I just want to see he is ok with my own two eyes." He starts ranting.

I grab him and pull him around and through the door to the stairs and slam him into the wall and snarl in his face "You ever speak like that in front of my son again and I will rip that tongue out of your fucking face and use it to slap you with. Do you understand?"

"Fuck you asshole. You could always try." At that he upper cuts me with a left jab which I return to his ribs and feel a few crack against my fist. Anyone who says that they can't feel things break against their fist are deluded.

He grunts and slides to the floor, he gets his wits about him and he grates out "She always was going to find someone to fight her battles. She picked someone with a good punch. So what made you fall for her? Was it the boy? Or was it her blowjob skills?"

Oh this fucker needs a lesson in respect "Neither. It was when she hit me with three hits and knocked me sleeping in my own ring while she had busted ribs and had gave birth not that long before. May I add she had busted ribs also due to her training to become what she is and that's the head of the familia. Have you happened to work out who the guy who raped her is yet? As I see the piece of shit, every time I walk into the club or watch through my scope when I am watching my Queen. Maybe you should be concentrating on that and not the fact that your wife has another man, one who will go through hell and back for her. Can you say that you would do the same Sparky can you? Do us all a favour and sign the divorce papers."

With that I turn and walk away. I can't be fucked with this wanker. As I walk through the door I see he is gutted. Guess he hasn't been home in a few days if he hasn't seen the papers.

"Never going to happen. No divorce. She is my wife and my ol lady. Get used to seeing my face, prick." He says just as the door latches shut.

He has some balls I will say that. But they are never going to be big enough to do anything to me or mine.

CHAPTER 6

SPARKY

Fucker broke my ribs. And fuck you very much, there will be no divorce. Treasure your ass is mine. I told her when she married me. I marry for life not for the moment. She knows this shit. Not my fault she didn't believe me.

She will soon though. First, down to the clubhouse and get these wrapped. Then, figure out who fucking raped and violated my Treasure. Surely it's not a brother. Can't be. No one would do that. Not to an ol lady, they are to be protected at all times. Never harmed. This is priority one after my ribs being sorted. I need to talk to Devil. Princess may have some clue. Although, surely she would have mentioned. Maybe I should just suck it up and ask Treasure. But I'm man enough to say I ain't doin' that. I will work it out it may take a day or 10 but someone will pay for touching my wife and ol lady.

Getting on my bike I know this is going to hurt like hell but it's my own fault for not winning. But next time, I'm going to kick his ass to get my woman.

The entire ride home I'm gritting my teeth and hoping I don't pass out. And trust me it's bad enough that it's a possibility.

Pulling into the clubhouse I see Devil is in along with what seems like half the club, at least the doc is here. I walk in sweat beading my head I walk up to the bar and ask for a whisky neat. Its fucking needed.

"Doc need you to wrap my ribs I have at least two broken. Don't ask just fix."

"What the fuck did you do this time brother?" Devil asks

"Got taught that my woman is in love with another man. As well as a few home truths. Will need a private word Pres. After. Stay sober as I need you will need a level head!"

He frowns and I can see he wants to know what's going on but I can't in a room full of brothers that I'm not entirely sure I trust as it could be one in this room. "Ok brother just find me after you are fixed. Yeah?"

"Yeah" I answer and head with doc to get my ribs fixed.

Lifting my head I see a few brothers smirking and Syco frowning and walking towards me.

"Need a word?" he asks with a look around the room.

Syco is the man that you never know what he is thinking hence his name. He originally got it because his first outing with the club as a prospect he was always muttering to himself. And while on that ride we stopped at a restaurant he spotted a guy that he swore he knew, turns out he didn't but he did see something we didn't if the beating that guy received was anything to go by. A week after that ride the guy got out the hospital and called him a psycho and the name stuck.

"Not yet brother but possibly, actually you are talkative with Treasure aren't you brother? Ever heard her talking about anything I should know?"

"Not here, brother not here. Your house? Yes. But that was before she left. You had me on watch that night. I didn't see but what she said pissed me off, that was why I never spoke to you for around a year. I'm now thinking that what I thought she meant wasn't what she meant."

"What? Brother what did she say? Why didn't you come to me all this time?" I grate out I just want to take my hands and wrap them around his throat until he spills everything and his blood.

Taking a calming breath I say "You know what tell me later I will send you a message and you can meet me after I get my ribs fixed. I feel like I'm breathing in knifes. Fucker needs an ass kicking of the highest fucking order."

He nods and turns his head to the side and says "I don't know who but I want a piece. And it was a brother. That's why I only speak to five brothers the rest I don't trust with a dime."

Shaking my head I limp to the back room where the doc is waiting this fucking sucks.

Seeing doc up ahead he smirks and says "Bullet or a punch?"

"Fuck you, just fix me none of your shit asshole." I snicker at him, knowing full well that he will either be in a good mood and take the piss back or be in a bad mood and make this hurt more than it already does.

He chuffs out a laugh and says "Was this Jess or was this the guy built like a tank? My bet is Jess I think she could easily hand you your ass on a silver platter"

Rolling my eyes. "Fix me and get to fuck doc, I've got too much shit to do and an ol lady to get back into my bed or her bed either or."

At that I feel him jab me with his finger right in the worst part of the pain. Fuckkkk me running.

I swig the bottle of whisky trying to drown out this pain. This shit must be watered down as its doing fuck all.

Just as I start to feel the effects of this drink hitting me Temp walks in "Yo brother how're the ribs?"

Ya'll are a bunch of nurse maids or gossiping bitches I'm just not sure anymore. I'm fine or I will be once everyone leaves me to get fixed up."

Temp doesn't move from his spot at the door. "Don't start bro. I want truth, how are you? How's Jessie and Simon." He asks

I turn fully to him and say with a deep frown "Why are you asking about my ol lady and my boy?"

He locks eyes with me like he didn't expect me to acknowledge Simon as my own. He may not be blood but he is mine just as she is mine.

"No reason brother, no reason." He about turns on his black military grade boots, and walks down the hall without looking back.

"Yo you weren't in the club the night Jessie left were you brother?" please say I'm wrong. Please don't be this motherfucker. I fought beside him for years since we joined the club.

He stops turns and nods his head winks and turns around and goes out the side door.

I'm fucking hating this, not knowing is bullshit. I need to know. I need to know who to kill for daring to hurt my ol lady not only hurting but to have raped her, well that deserves rusty spoon gouging eyes out and cocks being ripped off not cut off that's too nice for what this piece of scum deserves. He deserves only my best work.

Gritting my teeth I sit up and feel like I need some heavy duty pain killers. Fucking asshole!

Suck it up Spark time to go get shit done.

Getting off the bed I purposely walk through the door turn left down the hall and walk up the stairs. Whoever thought putting twenty-eight steps here needs an ass kicking of epic portions. All the way up these stairs I have bitched on every step.

At the top I stop and gain my breath then proceed to walk straight down the hallway, passing my room Craig's' room just as I'm passing Temps room I hear him moving shit then fling his door open and yank me through it and slam me into the wall. Shaking a few teeth loose by the feel of it, and now my ribs are screaming.

"What the fuck asshole!"

He leans in and says "Make it sound like we are fighting. This place has ears."

Nodding we start throwing shit at the walls and door and cursing until all goes quiet and we hear feet leave the hall. I am itching to know who had the balls to sit and wait for noise.

"Brother I was there, but you need to know that I have heard way too much fucking chatter. After I found out she was touched like that. I have had my eyes and my fathers' men's' eyes on everything, this afternoon I got word that we know who did it and my father won't give the name until he gets a meeting with his niece. Sparky brother, I'm sorry to say but that's Jessie. I have said we don't want Jessie to know we know. He has agreed that he will give us the information after he has spoken to Jessie."

He sparks up a cigarette and inhales deeply holds for a few seconds and releases his lung full with a plume of smoke.

"Brother I can't and won't have my ol lady involved. If she knew I was looking, I wouldn't hear the end of it. Fuck I wouldn't even get near her panties. I want in those again. Wait, how does your Dad not just message Jessie? Surely he could just say he wants to meet up for a meal."

"She doesn't know her uncle is alive. We are from her mothers' side. Not her fathers. When my dad found out my aunt, Jesses" mum, was killed, he did what he had always been told. Lay low build your house. That's what he has been doing, but when he heard what was going on with Jessie he has been on a tangent from hell. Normally he just allows me to do as I please without wanting me involved but not this time he has been demanding I work 'for the family' and sort this shit out. He originally didn't want her involved but after finding out what happened and who is involved he had to involve her. She is the family's' queen but she is 2 families queen. And we need her to know. So set it up. But make it like it's not her uncle, and don't fuck it up."

Well fuck me !

"I'm fucking speechless what am I supposed to do with that. She won't speak to me won't even look at me. So, I'm going to need more help than that."

An idea starts turning in my head, if only I could get Seb the dick on board.

"Actually brother I've got an idea." I walk away whistling.

CHAPTER 7

JESSIE

After getting home my first port of call was getting Simon into bed and to get a shower. Taking Simon to his bed after a quick bath where he decided to be back to his happy bouncy self. Not a lot knocks my boy off his happy world. I hated seeing him in that hospital and the fucking nanny is about to have an ass kicking from hell. Who the fuck gives a kid peanut butter without knowing if they are allergic. Ok I never even knew he was allergic but still.

After settling him in bed and giving him his huggle buggles I sing a lullaby and he drifts off.

By the time I have got to the end of the second line he is out like a light. Softly snoring, I swear he is just like me when I sleep, curls up on his left side one leg out of the cover and his pillow flung onto the floor within a second of sleep.

Chuckling to myself when he grunts as I open his door and allow light into the room, I step around the door and walk into Sebs arms, right where I need to be. In my man's arms.

"Jess we need a talk babe, nothing about us or Simon, something that I know you won't like, but babe.."

I stop him there "Seb I plan on going into our bedroom stripping naked walking into that shower having you get in with me and fucking me till I pass the fuck out with orgasms. Whatever the fuck you need to tell me can and will wait until the morning when I have had at least 7 hours sleep. Unless the planet is over run by fucking dinosaurs and aliens with probes on their heads I don't give a shit understood?"

He nods while obviously holding in a laugh.

"Good now move ass I want to sleep."

"Coming my Queen just as soon as I answer this call." He mutters towards his phone with a frown upon his face.

"Yeah?" he says as he walks down the hall and turns the corner towards the stairs.

As he gets to the stairs I hear "How the fuck did you get this number you piece of shit?"

Guess it's going to be a while and I won't be getting those orgasms then. Fuck it shower time.

I walk into my room with its plush soft white carpet and just stand in comfort and wiggle my toes in the carpet. This is why I spent more money on this carpet, for the fact that this is pure heaven in a carpet. Ok enough about my bloody carpet.

I start stripping off my top and drop it to the washing basket in the corner of the room next goes the bra then the bottoms then my panties and then I grab my towels from the dresser drawer and go into the bathroom where I turn the shower on and step in, enjoying the warm spray that hits my face as I step into the spray. I can't believe I need this shower so badly. But two days in the hospital was enough. Neither myself nor Simon like the hospital.

As I start to wash my hair I feel cold air hit my back and know my man has just walked into the shower. Just as a smile graces my face he wraps his arms around me and I can feel his hard thick long cock slide against my ass cheeks, and I shiver knowing my man is about to ravish my body with his and I can't fucking wait.

"Mmm my Queen is wet and not because of a shower. Have you been needing me gorgeous? Have you been needing my cock in this sweet pussy? The answer better be fucking yes as I'm about to slide him in this tight hole and give you my seed. Baby number two on the way."

"Babe don't! You know I'm still upset over the fact that I haven't given you a baby yet. Don't push the issue, just fuck me hard." I plead.

At that he pushes two fingers into my needy hole. I moan softly knowing he is going to tease the fuck out of me. I need him in me I don't want teased I want fucked until I can't breathe, I want him to wrap his hands around my throat and slightly squeeze, I want him to lose himself in my warm wet pussy. I need him like I need my last breath.

"Fuck! Seb please don't tease I need you way too fucking much to care about the tease. Just give me that cock of yours."

He chuckles and slams his dick home making me gasp with the force, if it wasn't for his firm grip on me I would have hit the floor of the shower.

"My Queen I'm about to fuck you sore." He grunts.

All I can feel is the sensation of his manhood sliding and grinding into me hard. He starts to speed up and be so much more forceful with his thrusts, feeling his breath on my neck and then his teeth scrape across my neck, sends shivers right through me, he is gripping my waist so hard I swear I can feel his bones, I need it harder and it's like he can read what I need as my orgasm builds and builds he grips the front of my throat and squeezes ever so slightly so that he isn't quite strangling me but I can feel my blood rushing through my ears. It's always been something that I wanted to do but no man ever wanted to do it until my King.

"Ahhh fuck. You're strangling my dick My Queen keep going let it release through you. Give me your rush. Fucking Cum!"

As he slams into me I let loose. I couldn't keep it at bay anymore if he kept this up I may just have died, yet he twists his hips and it's like I sail past bliss and straight into fucking heaven. I swear I go blind and when I come back down to earth he has me wrapped in a towel and laid on our bed. And I just know I went to my sexual space. I went into what I call my bubble. I know it's called sub space but I just don't like admitting I'm a sub. To be honest I have only ever been submissive with Seb.

CHAPTER 8

SEB

Catching her weight as she goes into her sexual bubble as she calls it, I get out carrying her wedding style and wrap her in a towel. I take her to our bed and sit down next to her when my phone chimes an unknown number

Unknown: We will arrive in the next 4 hours we will go to a hotel.

Me: Understood.

Seeing a message from the prick that is her husband

Prick: Have you told her? Has she given an answer?

He was the phone call that took me away from seeing my woman strip off her clothes and step into that shower without me.

He came up with a solution or in his mind it's a solution I just can't wait to see the fireworks from when I tell her his magical idea. When he told me my jaw hit the floor. Seriously what gave him the idea or the fact that I can't stand the prick. But fuck it. He can try to win her heart back. But he was told I am not going any fucking where. She is my Queen I am her king, and plus he needs someone as a buffer. I broke ribs she will break his dick I can't see him liking that, I may though.

Me: She is in her sex bubble. I will let her know when she wakes in the morning. I have other shit going on. Just find out who the fucker is in your goddamn club who hurt her and deal with him.

Prick: Sex bubble? Actually I don't want to know. I've got a meeting with the Pres will be over in the morning.

Me: No I have someone coming in the morning, she won't be at her best after they are here.

Prick: Fuck you I will be there at 8am get used to me asshole.

Me: Fuck you Prick. See you at 8 then but don't say I didn't fucking warn you.

I swear he is going to piss me off within a minute of being here tomorrow. Now to cuddle into my Queen and get some much needed sleep. Having my son in that hospital was horrible. I hate him being sick.

Although this was by peanuts not by anything else, the tests that he will need to go through sound lengthy but what my boy needs he will get.

Just as I am drifting off I get a message

Prick: Look I know we hate each other but she is my wife. I fucked up I know that but not a second has went by that I didn't think of my wife. She is also my ol lady and that is for life. So we need to at least be civil as we will both have her in our lives and will live together. Give it a chance and let both of us love her.

He is right and it fucking burns to admit but we do both love her.

Me: Ok be here for Breakfast at half 7. Bring your shit.

CHAPTER 9

SPARKY

Asshole: Ok be here for Breakfast at half 7. Bring your shit.

Scrubbing my face with my hand I take a deep breath. At least he is on board. Can't say my idea of just inserting myself back into her life is going to work but I'm an egotistical prick and she knows it. So she will most likely expect it from me.

I don't know how it will work with Seb but I'm willing to try and keep the peace if it means having my treasure back where she fucking belongs. A lot of people don't understand that when she disappeared it was like my heart disappeared along with her. My brothers all said I was a sap all said she was a two bit whore, yet none knew she never slept with any of the brothers.

Sure she partied but she was always around me. She hated leaving my side. I need to find out who this fucker is who hurt my Treasure.

Heaving myself off my bed I head to the door to go to Devils room when I hear a brother walking past I'm guessing on his phone as I never heard any other voices.

"She is back and by the sounds of it back to her usual ways. She obviously didn't take a telling last time maybe she needs a reminder, Need you to fuck him again and remember make it seem like you enjoy it bitch."

I open the door and grab the son of a bitch "Hi brother. Who pissed in your cornflakes this morning?"

"Ahh brother you know the girls who won't fuck off and stay away. I seem to have me one of those." Bobo says.

I just know this peace of shit is up to something. "Try brother. It's the worst thing for ya. Best get shot of her." I say but it tastes like shit is currently in my mouth.

"Don't I know it. She will be gone sooner than she thinks." And walks away with a smirk on his face.

Me: Keep an eye on her and Simon. Ask her about bobo.

If I'm not there I know he has her in his sight.

I lock my door and turn left and walk towards the door next to mine but two. I was fed up of hearing them fucking, swear it turned me off she is like a sister to me and hearing that yeah grossed me out.

I knock twice and devil shouts come in, "Are you dressed" I ask cautiously not making that mistake twice.

"Come in means come in fuck head yes we are decent"

"Can't be too careful Pres. Ok matters of business, someone raped my wife, it's a brother and I ain't sure who. She won't say to Seb and definitely won't tell me. Simon is the baby from that rape. I want the go ahead to take this fucker out when I find out who."

Straight out with it. "Oh and her uncle she doesn't know is alive wants a word and he will let us know information we need or tell us who I'm not quite sure which. Think that's about it. No no there's a little tidbit more, I'm moving in with her, Simon and Seb tomorrow morning she doesn't know so be ready to watch shit hit the fan."

Looking at both Devil and Princess you would have thought I just told them I was wanting to join a ballet company and dance in a dress. It wasn't that bad was it, I think I got it all out and it's not as bad as it would seem, ok Treasures shit is but hey ho and away we go.

"What? Wait what? I don't I mean I just, ok rewind there a minute one step at a time Sparks. She was raped by a brother?" Princess asks

"Yes"

Pulling out my phone I message Syco and Temps to head to Devils room.

"Who would dare touch another brothers ol lady?" Devil asks

"That's what I said, but it's got to be true. Can you remember all the times she is in the club, she has a sniper scoping the clubhouse and he doesn't let her out his sight, before you ask there is always a red dot on her. Always, and that's to show everyone that he has her in her sights at all times. I have watched that dot on her ass or right tit that many times that I think I know the make and model of the fucking thing." I growl out

"Spark we got the hint, but who would dare? Is she willing to tell us, or even Princess? We can't weed out the fucker."

"Well we can. I heard Bobo talking to someone and he is setting some guy up to get fucked by some bitch he knows by the sounds of it. I want eyes on that fucker as he was quick to tell me he has a bitch that has been causing him shit as she came back again. I ain't noticed anyone that was around before be back other than Treasure. I could be wrong but I need to get this meeting with her uncle underway which means I need to put myself in her way to make that happen. I need to hurt her to heal her do you know how fucked up that is, I yet again have to be the fucking bad guy. Ok the first time was my fault but she won't let me in and this is the only way I see it working with us. Pres I can't walk away from her she is my Treasure." I feel like my heart is about torn in two.

It has felt like it since she left, then when she came back with that asshole in tow I thought she was deliberately trying to hurt me. Until a few days ago I still thought that, seeing him and her together made me realise that I was being a complete wanker. If I don't step up and be her husband and ol man, I'm about to fully lose my wife and ol lady and that shit just won't happen.

Tomorrow come 7 am she will be seeing my things in drawers in her room and my shit in bathrooms and kitchens and a new fucking television as hers is way too fucking small.

I know of two others in that house that will appreciate the upgrade come football and hockey season.

I can't wait for the fireworks from my ol lady when she sees my ass in her house tomorrow morning. And knows I won't be leaving.

Smirking Devil answers the knock at his door, "I'm in a meeting brothers what's needed?"

"Pres we are here for the meeting" Syco says

He walks up to me fist bumps me and sits next to me on the couch. Temp stays near the door doing his job keeping an ear out.

"Pres I knew something happened with Jess but not who done it, originally I thought this fuck head done it but recently found out it wasn't him, I don't know who but I want in on finding the bastard and putting him to ground." Syco said all this with the biggest smile on his face, this man scares the shit out of me on a good day and he is one brother I wouldn't like to piss off.

"And I'm her cousin but she doesn't know it. My father, her uncle did what was told of him when her mother was killed, and that was to get his house in order and stay clean. That's what he did, but now he needs to talk to her, he says he knows who done it but is unwilling to share until he has a word with Jessie. If I'm honest I don't trust it, I don't trust him. I never have Pres no one knew why I refused to work with the family but he is demanding I do, and that's why I don't trust the bastard. After seeing what I did when I was a child, I can't in all good conscious let him be close to her without an army surrounding her." Temp spits out that last bit.

What the fuck happened when he was a kid?

CHAPTER 10

SYCO

Never again, never again, never again. These words are the words I mumble. And I don't mean to mumble. The day that Jessie heard me mumble those words was the day she was raped by a so called brother. Jessie was my friend or I liked to think she was. She was and still is the only woman who doesn't look at me as if I'm a psycho. Ok, Princess just lets me get on with it but there is the times' she looks at me worriedly. I'm guessing that's the times she goes back into her shell and doesn't want a lot of people barring Devil around.

I never knew who raped Jessie but I want to be there when they catch and kill the piece of shit.

I also wouldn't mind finding someone that looks at me like Jessie secretly looks at Sparky. She may not admit it she may fight it fight him but she still loves that man. She may also love Seb but she will always love Sparky. Nothing wrong with loving more than one person. Although one would be enough for me, if only there was someone strong enough to love me, strong enough to want the scarred and scary freak of the club.

I'm bitching I know, but I can't help what happened and why I mumble, why I keep away from everyone. Pres knows but that's thanks to a lot of drink and him telling me to speak up when he thought I was talking to him.

I start trying to rake my memories about the night Jessie came home scratched up crying and limping.

TWO YEARS AGO

I've hauled my ass up to Jessie and Sparkys house for watch, I may not be a prospect but it keeps me away from the looks.

I watch as Jessie's car flies into her space in front of the house. She is limping and looks like she has been hurt. What the fuck?

Just as I go to ask her what has happened she breaks down and screams.

"How could he? How could any man do this to a woman, to me?? I thought he was one of the good ones. Guess I'm wrong."

She paces between the kitchen and the living room, I'm stuck to my spot. It sounds like she has been, and I don't want to jump to conclusions but, it seriously sounds like she has been raped. She stops dead in front of the living room window which is open and says

"I need to pack, I need to leave. I need my family. I am so glad no one knows who I really am, specially Princess."

Do I stop her do I let her go??

I phone Sparky he should know. Wait what if it was Sparky? I need to phone someone. I know I will phone my cousin. He will have an idea of what to do.

I dial his number answering with "Yo cuz, what's wrong?"

"Ok so my friend I think has been raped and I don't know by who, but it could also be her ol man, and she has just said to herself, she is going to her family. Do I let the ol man know? Do I chance that it may be him and she will get more of this treatment? What do I do Shane?"

"Deep breath Bryan deep breath. Let me have her email and her phone number and her name. I will keep an eye on her. Sounds like her ol man either done it, doesn't know or doesn't care. But surely she would have phoned or went to him?" he asked.

That there made me think I'm not telling him shit sparky can find out that his ol lady left himself.

And he did six days later. Six fucking days to realise she wasn't there.

All because he was that drunk and drugged up he didn't care about anyone bar himself. From that day on I was positive he done it, I was adamant that he raped and harmed Jessie, yet had the utter balls to say he was upset his Treasure left him. Really well he was happy to fuck women in the club when he wanted it so wasn't that broken up about it, he was happy to drink and snort everyday while she was away.

The day she walked back in those doors was the day I smiled again after nearly two years. Two years I've missed her face. And she saw me first and ran full tilt into my arms, which may I add no one touches me never mind runs into my arms.

Catching her and spinning her round while squeezing her tight she whispers

"Thank you for having your family watch out for me, he wasn't all busy hiding himself. I know a tracker when I see one, but thank you. He says hi and to visit."

I whisper back "I fucking missed you Jessie. Are you ok?"

"I'm good yeah. I need to step away or Seb won't be happy if the dot on your shoulder is anything to go by."

I look at my right shoulder and sure enough I have a red scope on my shoulder. Looking through the window up above where I sit I wave at that my phone rings with an unknown number.

"Hello"

"If you want to keep your arms keep them away from my Queen"

"Tut tut you're asking for a dance and I don't even know your name. Gimmie the name of my dance partner and I shall think on it some more."

"Fucking hell I know she called you Syco but I didn't think you were actually a psycho, just introducing myself I want a meet at her house tonight if you can manage it. Names Seb, may as well keep you in the loop. She trusts you don't be a bastard and make her loose her trust in the only person outside of the family. Or I will destroy you for hurting her."

"Clear on that one." And I hang up.

Turning to Jessie I ask "Are you here for good?"

She nods and looks like she has went white as a sheet. I look around seeking what made the change and I see that a good number of the brothers have walked in. If I could pinpoint what one it is that hurt her I would happily put a bullet in them. But there is too many. Hence the factor why I only trust a few brothers in this chapter.

"You are now family surely Shane told you that. I will protect you all you need to do is let me be there. Always Jessie always."

She smiles and looks at me "Well I may need to tell you there's another two people to add to that list Shane knows though. My man Seb and my son Simon. Thank you for being you Syco thank you for being there the night I left and including me into the family. Never thought I would like the Irish accent, but Shane is dreamy to listen to."

Yeah I am definitely not telling him that, he already has a big head. The prick.

I am glad I let my cousin be involved in Jessie, if it wasn't for him keeping in touch I don't know how I would have felt. He kept me a little more sane with his updates over the years.

"Why are you here?" I ask.

"To protect Princess and to make somebody's' life a living hell until I kill him." And with that bombshell she walks off towards the bar. Let the shit hit the fan then sister of mine.

That was the day she became an even bigger part of my life, she became my sister not just a family member.

CHAPTER 11

SPARKY

Looking over at Syco who is currently sitting with a smile on his face even though we are discussing who could have raped my ol lady. Kinda creepy kinda pisses me off. I nudge him and he looks over and raises his eye brow at me.

"Quit the smiling. It's wrong on so many levels." I mutter to him

He looks at me as though I'm the strange one "What the hell are you talking about? I'm not smiling, I was remembering something that happened. Maybe that was it. Probably to be honest. Ah well. Back to it brother."

If he wasn't a brother I would be worried about peoples' safety. As it is I don't want him near my family, but I also trust him with my life. And Treasure seems to be attached to him, same as that asshole Seb. I really need to stop calling him an asshole. No I don't, won't be able to.

"Look brother we need to decide how we proceed. Do you want Jessie to meet her uncle and get this information, or is it a case of she is kept out of the loop and we make it as though her uncle just wants to know her? This is all on you." Devil asks

I look at him and I mean really look at him for some sort of clue as to what I should do. Seeing him become happier yet so much more defensive of not only Princess and his family, but the club as well. For years he has been our Pres and has always defended us nearly with his life for fuck sake. But he is so much more stronger with his family at his side.

I turn and stare into the mirror at myself and take a hard look at myself, never been one to give a shit about my looks. But seeing my light blue eyes the square jaw line and that fucking scar below my eye that runs in a straight horizontal line from my nose to just before my ear. Seeing the dark brown almost black hair and all I can imagine in the mirror standing by my side is my Treasure. My Jessie looking at me as though I'm her world and knowing she wouldn't want me to lie to her.

When I cheated on her with Melissa I was that out my mind with coke that I didn't even know it wasn't Jessie, I thought I was seeing double until I realised what the fuck was happening. But if I'm honest with myself, I thought I was a fucking king. I had my gorgeous ol lady I had my club I had the world in my hands, until I didn't. When Jessie left I fell into a shitty hole and it took Princess appearing to pull me out of it.

SIX MONTHS AFTER JESSIE LEFT

Yet again I feel like I'm on top of the fucking world. I feel like I should be the happiest man in the world. But I'm not. My treasure isn't here and she just fucking up and disappeared, not one word. As I have Alys' hot snatch grip my hard rigid cock as she bouncing up and down my shaft, letting me see what I swear is six tits but knowing in my head is only two sway and bounce with her movements, I know I'm supposed to actually be enjoying this but I can't.

It isn't until I imagine my Treasure that I begin to feel like I should be enjoying this and once her image is in place of this bitch I feel my balls tighten and I know my ol lady is going to fuck me until I explode and feel like the cum will never stop pumping out of me.

"Ahhh fuck me Treasure. That's it Jessie take it take what you need, fucking take what you need. Fucking ride me baby" I roar out as I feel like I am about to release all my seed into her tight wet pussy.

"What the fuck!? It's Aly you asshole" is screamed and that is like a bucket of cold water with ice flung over me.

Gripping her hips I fling her off me. "Get out of here, slut! My treasure will not see me with you."

She looks like I have lost my goddamned mind, which I guess I have. Getting off the bed disgusted with myself I walk in to the bathroom to the right of my room and just make it to the toilet where I throw up and feel like I am bringing up all the chemicals all the drugs in my system and I can't fucking breathe. That's when I wipe my mouth and remember she left, she left six months ago and I haven't asked anyone to look for her. I haven't even tried, I've not asked around in case she is just not wanting to talk to me. Although I know. I fucking know down to my bones that something other than me cheating on her is the reason she left. I think that's why I'm afraid, yes fucking gutless bastard that I am, I am too fucking afraid to ask as I know something happened. And me being too busy being a selfish bastard, hasn't looked or even found out why she left.

I haven't been to our house, I have hardly left the club other than the runs that are on rotation. I know that we have someone here we have to take care of and that we are being paid fucking handsomely for that but I don't know who when or where.

I drag myself across the ice cold black tiles to my black and silver shower. As I get the strength to pull myself up I reach up and turn the shower on and just drop hard onto my knees, I feel them scrape across the tiles and know I've made them bleed, yet I don't care. It's like a fucking dam breaks and all I can do is sob. And not fucking quietly. Its gut retching, I feel like I've broke and nothing will put me back together. I feel two arms surround me and I swear it feels like it's only those arms holding me together.

"Shhh nothing can be that hard, nothing can't be fixed. I've watched you around and it's like you held everything together too tight, as though you also didn't believe anything could happen to you. Sparky, it's time to fix it. I don't know what it is, no one will talk to me other than Devil, who incidentally wouldn't left me in here without him as soon as I heard you hit the floor to be sick. The big bastard is behind us holding me holding you, lets' not tell the other brothers he listened to a bitch shall we, can't make him lose man card points." Princess whispers in my ear.

She is the one who made me take my foot out of my ass and find my ol lady. Ok I couldn't, it was as though she fucking vanished, so much so I actually began to think she had died. That was until Princess took off and then there was certain things that made me feel as though she had eyes on me all this time.

That was fucking laughable, as if she had the fucking people who could do that.

Turns out, that's exactly what happened. She did have men keeping watch, but not on me, oh no that's not true. Not just me. Princess, Syco and the fucker who raped her.

PRESENT DAY

"Let her know Pres. I'd prefer not to be killed by her if she was to ever find out I didn't let her know." I give him a look that I hope to god he understands.

He nods his head saying "Ok brother, set up a meeting with us all at her house tomorrow."

Temp sits up straighter and shakes his head saying "Pres I have a run tomorrow we will need to make it another day."

I look over at him, frowning I think we don't have a run tomorrow.

"There are no runs tomorrow brother what are you talking about." Pres asks

"It's personal Pres, but needs to be done tomorrow morning may take me into the night, depending on the happenings of the day." Temp has his eyes diverted from us. Something ain't right, I fucking knew something wasn't right. Hopefully it's his family shit and not club shit.

"Hey brother we can wait on you, will make it for the day after tomorrow how's that for everyone?"

Nods all around the room are received and as I smile I see that Syco has left the room. "Where the fuck did Syco go?"

Blank stares and Princess quietly stating "He…he said he had to go in my ear." She is shaking like a mother fucking leaf. What the fuck just happened?

Shaking my head I go to leave and hear a ping in my pocket. Pulling it out it's from Princess.

Princess: blood will flow within the month. Things are not as they seem, not everyone is who they seem. Dig deep and find the truth brother. I will spill first blood, just you be there to protect your ol lady, my sister or you will be the one I kill, brother or not.

What in the fuck? I turn to look over at her and she has those bloody eyes on me as if I'm supposed to know what that shit means. Wait, she said Syco said he had to go, is this from him?

CHAPTER 12

DEVIL

After everyone left my room, Princess is fiddling with the sleeve of her sweater. I know she had words with Syco but she looks like she has seen a ghost. It's the first time she has actually spoke to Syco and Temp, so could just be her having an anxiety attack. I saw that Syco spoke quietly to her, but he wouldn't fuck with her while I was right in front of him, and he may seem like a strange one but he is one of my best men. I trust him with my life.

Something has set her off and I want to let her get through the attack and then I will calmly ask what the fuck is going on.

I move to my right and pull her towards me and she instantly melts into me.

Kissing the top of her head I ask "What's wrong Princess?"

Watching her chest rise and fall and I'm loving the view. These tits of hers are double the size they were. "Something Syco said makes me think that we may be closer to the rapist than we think. Devil I won't have someone like that in the club and around my kids. I want this bastards head. He has made me have to face a fucking fear and talk to Syco. That man freaks me out, which ok I may possibly be like that because he is strange but not the point. I've just went through an anxiety attack I hate them. I feel like I can't breathe I feel like I'm having a heart attack. Right now I'm clammy as hell. Until this is dealt with I'm going to see if I can visit with Angel. The kids and I will come home when it's sorted, and I'm not freaking out if the prick is close to us and can do that shit to me or hurt the kids."

My frown is firmly in place "Fuck you Princess. Take care of you? Take care of my kids? Are you fucking kidding me?"

I get up and storm out the room and down the stairs as I get to the bottom one my phone vibrates in my back pocket. Whoever it is can fuck off I need a beer.

As I slam through the door of the bar, heads lift and know not to approach me, other than Bull. Of course someone has to be stupid enough to approach, even Princess has left me alone and she is always first to follow and chew me out.

"Yo Pres what's up your ass? Princess not dropping those panties anymore? Fancy a run to the strip club? It's been ages since you partied with us." He stupidly asks.

I slam my hand on the sticky wet bar top. "Get me a fucking drink and a wet cloth. Are we pigs in this club? Can't fucking clean up after yourselves?" I shout.

"Take that as a no Pres. Maybe you need to pin that bitch down and sink deep. She is your ol lady. Maybe it's time to show her that she needs to do what you say and just take it."

Not a millisecond after he says his last word is my fist swinging towards his face. As it connects and blood sprays from his mouth I roar out, "Don't fucking talk about my ol lady like she is a whore."

I keep punching him as I hold him up by his shirt. It takes five brothers to pull me off him, but it's not until I hear Princess scream from the direction of the kitchen that I snap out of it.

Myself and the five brothers charge into the kitchen to see her on the floor with a small smear of blood on the floor under her and her holding her upper arm with blood seeping through her fingers.

Blood rushes through my ears "Princess what happened?"

She gets off the floor and walks toward the cupboard under the sink and retrieves the first aid kit. She brings it back to the table with a blank expression.

"Well Husband of mine. I walked in here after seeing you kicking the shit out of one of the brothers, you know leaving you to get the anger out, decided I would make something to eat as I put down the bread I just lifted from the cupboard on the way in. I get shot. In my own home. Where you know the kids are safe. Where I'm safe." She says all this so detached and its fucking scary. I know this has just cemented the fact that she is taking the kids to Angel until this has been sorted.

"Now Princess you know this will have been a one off, no need to completely shut down here, nice deep breath. I will find the shooter and deal with him myself. But do not do anything rash."

She starts to giggle then full out laugh while she is cleaning the wound meticulously. It takes her a while but after she is back to softly laughing she pulls her phone out and I know she is messaging Angel. "Devil, don't do anything rash? I have to not do anything rash. Have I got that right? I have just had a bullet go in and back out my upper arm, right now it fucking hurts, but I have to calm down take a breath and not do anything rash. Not only that but I am sitting here in pain fixing myself as six, no make that seven men and a fucking dog look on. Although the dog is actually sitting under the table watching me like I'm about to hit the floor at a drop of a hat, yet my own fucking husband says don't do anything fucking rash. Oh we are so past rash that I can't begin to explain how rash shit has just got." She is staring holes through me and I know I just royally fucked up.

"Princess if you want to take the kids and yourself to Angels then that's fine I understand, but I need to take care of you and I don't want you killing me with the knife you currently have in your hand with a death grip." Yes I am fucking scared right now, she is a fucking hellcat when she starts.

"I'm not going anywhere. I want this little piece of shit who shot me. The kids though, they are leaving in the next 27 minutes. I'm now going to wrap this and pack the kids up and give them all my hugs and kisses. I would advise you do also. They will not be back until we sort this new shit. Then I want a fucking month without one fucking incident, and you best believe I mean that. If there is one fucking problem in a month heads will roll. Is this understood?" all around me heads nod.

"Who is coming for them?" I cautiously ask

"Daddy."

Fuck!

CHAPTER 13

JESSIE

I wake up look at the clock that is glowing green and it reads 07.11. I didn't hear Simon and Seb isn't in bed with me. I slide my hand to his side of the bed and feel it's cold, stretching and enjoying the fact I don't have a small child in with me. Which on its own is scary. It's so strange but feels so good to have a bed to myself. Just as I feel comfortable I find myself looking at the dresser.

Frowning thinking I must be seeing things. There is a bottle of men's' Burberry weekend on my dresser along with a new lamp that is most definitely not mine. I can remember the thing but I can't remember the last time.... Oh fuck no! I jump out of my bed fling the door open not caring I'm in small shorts and a bra top.

I storm down the hall muttering that I best not have seen what I think I have seen and if this bastard is in my house then I'm going to kill the prick along with Seb for allowing this to happen.

Getting to the stairs I take them two at a time. Nearly falling at the last two steps I storm down the hall and get to my kitchen door and open it slowly, just in case Simon is behind it, seeing that he isn't, I walk up behind this scummy shit head who dares to situate himself in my house, technically it is both ours but still not the point, he just moved his stuff in, into my room. Mine not his mine!

"Who the hell do you think you are putting your crap in my house? Never mind the bloody house but in MY room." Turning to Seb I snap out "Did you know about this? Did you just let him do it?"

Seb gets away from the sink and stalks towards me "My Queen we didn't have a choice, he does own the house with you. He has rights. And yes I did know as I agree with him, Jess you both need to talk. But you only have about 30 minutes until people start coming over. I will say I did let him not wake you. You can be pissed all you want but, he is your husband. If you wanted rid of him you would have divorced him, and you would have sold the house. Maybe time to admit you still love him. Just like you love me." And he just walks out the kitchen shouting Simon that it's time to get dressed.

 Walking to the kettle I make myself my morning coffee, right now it's needed. I'm not ready for this conversation. I know he is going to ask what happened and why I didn't talk to him, why I never filed for divorce. And the answer to all of those are I don't know don't want to talk to him about it and that yes if I am completely honest with myself I do still love this big dickhead. But I'm not going to say that to him, pfft no chance and let him preen and rub it in my face that he and Seb were right. Fuck that I will never hear the end of it.

Sitting down directly across from him I look at him while he stares at me like I've broke him. Maybe I did but my spies told me that he has happily been fucking the same girl for a year. But do I believe them or do I trust that he may have but he hasn't been with anyone since I appeared back. And that I know for certain.

He takes a breath and speaks "Treasure are you willing to talk civilly?"

With that one word I fucking break. Hearing the word Treasure come out of his mouth just made it all seem more real. I know that sounds so weird and wrong but he was the only man that has ever called me that. I am his treasure and he was too busy fucking another woman while I was being violated by his brother. I was being damaged while he was in the building I was outside of. It was 43 minutes of hell while he was most likely finished in 10 minutes and then happily oblivious having a beer and having a laugh with his brother, the brother that sits with him daily who has the gall to say to him he is helping find himself. I can't put up with this.

"No, I'm not. But I have to. When you were with Melissa after I saw you I left out the back room. I went to go walk along the path that runs along the lake. I got about twenty steps away from the door when I was slammed against the wall at the back of the clubhouse. Slammed so hard I lost consciousness for about three minutes, just enough time to be stripped of my trousers and panties. He said to me 'He can fuck who he wants, like he's the big man. Like he is a fucking God. Well I'm about to show him he ain't all that. You bitch are a message, to more than one person.'

He destroyed me Sparks utterly destroyed me. Every push and pull every punch and the absolute worst was when Bobo walked out and was no less than twenty fucking steps away and didn't do anything. Didn't look was too busy with a whore on her knees sucking his cock. And you wonder why I have Seb with a laser and a gun on me keeping an eye out. I still can't hate the club, I can't even hate Bobo, there has only been one person who looked out for me that night. After he raped me and then punched me so hard that he broke my teeth and my nose. I went home and I was going to wait until the morning and talk to you but I couldn't face you and possibly have you look at me like it was something that was all on me, or worse on you. I didn't want to cause shit between you and the club. What I didn't know was Syco was on watch, he saw me come home he saw me breakdown and he heard what I said. What he did was get in contact with his family and asked them to take care of me, keep an eye on me. And I can't be more thankful for what he did. I call him my brother, he is part of my family. He was there when I needed him. The one thing you need to know is he never knew where I was. I would send his cousin an email to let him know what was going on but when I came back he was there, he told me that nothing would harm me and that he would die before he allowed anyone to harm me again." I'm trying so hard not to continue crying. It is too hard, I can't tell him this and look at him so I look at my table.

Looking at the salt grains on the table I concentrate on them, I see where the plate was when Seb put salt on his plate I see that he must have used the square plate, my good plates.

I need to concentrate to get the rest of this out, Sparks is so quiet that I wish he would speak, this silence is not good. I don't know if he is angry at his brother or if it is disgust with me. It took a long, long time to realise that the rape was not my fault. I didn't do anything to make him do it. I didn't deserve it. No one deserves to go through that. No one has the right to harm another.

Taking a deep breath I continue.

"I got in my old car, the one I knew didn't have any GPS tracker in it, and drove a state over and got on a plane to my Father. I needed my daddy. He wanted blood for what happened, but he was happy to let me handle it. The night I arrived I was taken to my fathers' friend who fixed me up and got me in contact with a counsellor. I made sure that it would be a man so I made sure that I wasn't going to find a fear of men. Exactly seven weeks after I arrived home with my father I was feeling rough and thought no I can't be, this hasn't just created life? It did, my son is the product of a rape. My son will NEVER and Sparks I mean fucking never know that, he doesn't need to. If he ever asks then I will happily lie to my son and say his dad died. Which I will make sure, technically, won't be a lie.

I gave birth and he is the most precious thing in my life, just looking into those dark blue eyes and I melted, here he was I couldn't name him. It wasn't until I looked at him without the tears in my eyes and he was asleep that I named him."

I got up and walked into the pantry to pick up the photo albums of the first three weeks of my Simon's life and walked back to the table sat down, opened the first page and took out the very first photo that I personally took.

"This is Simon about an hour maybe a little more old. This is why I named him after you. He sleeps the exact same way you do. Hand under his jaw tongue against his bottom lip and a small sigh when he is fully asleep and happy. I cried my heart out knowing that as much as he reminded me of you, he sadly wasn't yours. We hadn't had sex in over two weeks because you were too busy fucking Melissa, since she was new. And before you ask or even try and deny it, I walked in every single day at the worst possible time. I even heard you tell her she was tighter than anyone you ever had. That was something you once told me. That fucking hurt Sparks hurt fucking bad. But I stupidly still never left you and do you know why? Because I'm a fucking mug and I love you. I still love you Sparkus but I also need you to understand I love my King, I love Seb."

I sat there waiting on him to speak, it took so long that I actually thought he left while I was talking. I chanced looking up and I wish I knew what he was thinking.

He was sitting in front of me with a look of despair, of utter heartbreak. He was staring at Simons picture. He cleared his throat

"I want a dna test. You say he is definitely not mine but looking at him here and seeing him properly this morning I don't believe he isn't mine. I understand you don't think he is mine but dates can be wrong. Did you give birth to him early or on due date?" he looks at me when he says that last bit.

Replying I say "He was a month early but healthy was only kept in because he was early. But as I said scans and everything else pointed towards not being your child. Sparky you need to keep that in mind, you can't go off when you find out that everything I am saying is the truth. You may want him to be your son, but he isn't. If by some miracle I'm wrong doctors midwifes are wrong then I will apologise."

"Who is it? Who dared to harm one fucking hair on your head? Jessie you need to tell me, you need to let someone know. What if he does that to another ol lady? Can you live with that?"

"Fuck you! I am protecting your fucking club. I am protecting the ol ladies by making sure my men fucking follow him like a Hawk. He has other backing. I just need to figure out who the fuck the big wig is. The rape was to hurt more than the club."

He is shaking his head and shouts "Just fucking tell me who the fuck raped you. You are my fucking life, I did you wrong when I was cheating. Fuck sake I didn't even realise I was cheating as I was too busy being fucked out of my head on coke. I thought the whores were you. I came home every fucking day to a cooked meal and my wife asleep in bed ready for our nightly cuddles after I fucked her hard in the club. If you spoke up I would have took notice. I would have known I was doing wrong. What else did you think. Did you really think I would harm you that way? I love you Treasure you are my treasure my world my fucking everything. Once I came out of my drug induced shithole, I realised I needed to find out what the fuck made you run. And I knew you ran as there was not one item of clothing touched the only things you took were your passport your fucking unicorn purse and our wedding photo. That's how I knew something must have happened, and the most important part that kept me going, kept me fucking hunting the fucking earth for you was the fact you took that picture and that you still loved me as that was the one thing you said would always keep you going if I ever died in the club. Was our wedding day and how special it was when you married your soul mate."

He has tears tracking down his cheeks and I wish I could tell him who, but I need to find out what he is up to, and that's not even for me, it's for the club. To keep the club safe. To keep all the brothers safe all the ol ladies all the kids safer than if they were wrapped in cotton wool and bubble wrap and stored in the largest safe known to mankind.

"I would like to know that also." Is said, by a woman who is standing in my doorway. I snap my head up and I'm looking into the eyes of my Mother. What the hell. Before I can even think it's all too much and I feel like I can't breathe, I feel like I'm about to have a heart attack and black out.

CHAPTER 14

SPARKY

Jumping up and grabbing Jessie before her body hit the floor and caused damage. I cradle her in my arms and tap her cheek and say "Treasure come on babe, Treasure open up those peepers for me."

Her guest kneels down and runs her hand through Treasure's hair while softly saying "Marko bring me the smelling salts, knew this would happen. Although I didn't expect to hear all this that's been going on."

Marko makes a non-committal noise and hands her, her bag.

"So is someone going to explain what the fuck has been going on with my daughter, and why the fuck I haven't been informed?" she is busy rummaging through her black massive looks like a fucking Mary Poppins bag with the way she is nearly elbow deep in it.

"Sofia we were ordered not to inform you as it would make you come out of hiding, and I'm sorry to say but word is family is involved or at least are nearby. Jess has been seeing a councillor once a month. And if I am totally honest I have not heard all of the story until just now. I cannot apologise enough that she wasn't protected but we weren't entirely sure of where she ran to." Seb says.

Wait does that mean Seb has known her all along, which means he lied to her and if she finds out I know from experience she will be pissed beyond pissed.

"Seb I don't care, she is my child I left to protect the family. And now, now I see that she is in more danger than she should be. What member of the family is here? And have they had a hand in this shit?" Sofia rapidly asks.

Its silent in the kitchen until Simon shouts "Mama, Mama, Mama"

It's like she was just sleeping in her bed and had a five minute nap. Jessie snaps awake and sits straight up pushing her mother away and smiles at Simon.

"Hello my gorgeous baby boy. Have you had breakyfast? "

He sticks his thumb in his mouth and shakes his head, the sneaky little poop, he had pancakes along with us. Oh if he gets more pancakes I will be demanding more, it's been about three years since I had my ol lady's pancakes.

"Hmmm are you sure? Because I can see some syrup on your cheek. Do you just want some more? What about you mum? Pancakes uncle Marko? Ok pancakes for breakfast. Since you are staying now Sparks go take my son my mother my uncle and Sebastian into the living room and entertain yourselves. Actually no I think me and Simon will make some pancakes and the rest of you can go and talk in the living room please. Food will be ready in 20 minutes." She speaks so calmly which is fucking scary as it usually means someone is about to hear her roar.

"Ok baby we can do that. Give a shout if you need anything" I say and gesture to the rest to follow me.

As we all go to leave Seb is looking like someone just destroyed his whole world. I nudge his shoulder and whisper "Trust me give her time to get her bearings, once she does she will talk or kick somebody's ass." I pat him on the shoulder and he follows me out the door.

"She called me Sebastian, she never calls me that. She was so detached and that isn't how she normally is. Don't you think someone should be in there with her?" he looks back at the door, he must have a shit load going through his head to be thinking all that. The woman needs a little time to wrap her head around the fact that her mother has just walked through her front door after how many years, never mind that she also just finished breaking down to me which I'm not even close to fucking processing so I'm just letting her have that breath that she needs. Plus Syco is right outside, she won't go far. Syco watches her like she is spun glass.

"Seb trust me just leave her for a bit, she is in shock. How would you feel if the mother you though was dead has just walked into your kitchen? Let her process her way."

He nods but still looks like someone took away his toy. Time to entertain the in-laws I guess.

"Hi I'm Sparky, your daughters husband and ol man." I say sticking my hand out. Her uncle Marko grabs my hand to shake and promptly slams his head into mine bursting my nose. Lovely first meeting. Not one to hold back I throw a punch with my right and connect to his jaw, at that he starts to laugh and says "You'll do. Welcome to the family now tell us what the hell is going on?"

"Too much shit but my Pres is coming over in around two hours for a catch up." looking around to speak to her mother I can't see her in the room.

"Where is Sofia?" I ask

"With Jess I guess." Marko replies.

CHAPTER 15

JESSIE

After everyone leaves the kitchen I nod out the window to Syco. Watching him push off the old oak tree that's in my garden, I try and sort my mind out. What the fuck is going on. Plastering a smile on my face for Simon I turn and ask him what he wants for eating and as I take a look at him I burst out laughing.

My lovely baby boy is sitting where I sat him in his high chair, but he has pulled the flour over to him and must have slapped his hands against the bag and a puff of air has come out and he is covered in flour. I have to take a photo and send it to Princess. He is just too precious. My boy always makes me smile, no matter how shitty of a day I have had he always puts shit into perspective.

As I go over to clean my son I see that my mother is standing in the door way with a smile on her face. That face that I have missed for seven years, my family lied to me for years. Thinking back to when I last saw those blonde curls that perfectly shaped face those sparkling blue eyes. And that broken nose that I gave her when I was a toddler. When oi start to remember that as much as I missed the hell out of my mother, she lied. She made me believe she was dead when I needed her the most. I can't forgive her for that.

"I asked you all to go to the living room. As much as that was asked politely right now I'm about as close to losing my shit, especially with you mother. Go to the living room, breakfast will be ready soon."

She shakes her head with a smile on her face. "That shit you got from your father. Certainly not from me. I would be kicking my ass for lying. And I'm guessing that breakfast is currently all over my adorable grandson, I'm sorry I wasn't here to help bring him into the world. Jessicka there are things that you need to know about why I had to be made out to be dead. But knowing the look of disgust on your face I know you don't care. But lady you will listen when I speak. This all relates to what you are taking over. I'm not stepping back in this pile of shit, but I will help guide you and help with my grandson."

She is staring at my son with tears in her eyes and it is seen that she has missed a lot but I don't care for people who are fucking assholes to be involved in my sons life. She faked her own death from me, her own child. No one thought that I deserved or could be trusted enough to know she was alive.

"Did my father know you are alive? If it wasn't for walking in and seeing my fathers mutilated body trussed up for the fucking world to see I would be thinking is he alive and faking it too."

I'm livid beyond belief. But I'm really trying to keep myself steady for my son.

She looks at me directly and states "He did. It was his idea to keep us all safe. Either I 'died' or my family would kill you. I stand by my decision Jessicka that will never change. You are my world my sun my moon my stars, my blood. I would do anything to keep you safe. But right now that isn't going to happen and I fucking pray that it isn't your uncle my brother that is in this area, because if he is we are both going to have to deal with him and I mean in a permanent way. This is a discussion for later though, now who is your friend?"

I frown and turn seeing that Syco has walked in the back door and is now sitting next to Simon and is cleaning him up.

"Syco, ma'am nice to meet you. Jess there's things happening and we need to talk once Pres and

Princess appear. Breakfast first though I'm starving."

I can't help but laugh my Syco will always be hungry when I'm cooking. He could have ate two giant steaks and walk in this house see me making a meal to feed forty and demand I make him double. He is a human bucket.

"Syco you know I make you double so less of that please. Keep cleaning your Nephew and I will cook. Mum can entertain herself or meet her grandson. His name is Simon just so you know mum" I say.

For the next half an hour no one speaks to me although I can feel their eyes on me. I make stack after stack of Pancakes knowing that Devil and Princess are coming and no bloody doubt want them as well. It's relaxing for me to cook specially pancakes as it's just repetitive and stops my mind from wandering. Grabbing the square pale grey plates from the middle shelf of the third cupboard along I start plating up. Counting in my head.

Simon two pancakes. Syco eight pancakes. Sebastian six pancakes. Sparky six pancakes and two toast. Mum four pancakes. Uncle Marko six pancakes. Me two pancakes one toast. Syrup and chocolate sauce on the table. Coffee on. Orange juice and water on table ten forks on table.

I'm not sure if cooking was my best idea as my mind is whirling with what the fuck is actually going on. Why people won't just tell me this shit. It's not like I'm a fucking wallflower or such a girlie girl that I will run away screaming and not dealing with shit. Ok I ran from my rape but it was not just for my mind it was for sparks the club and family that I have made here. I didn't want them being hurt.

It already looks like I broke Sparky and I never wanted that. I am alive some men and women who go through what I went through and worse took their own lives, or couldn't pull through the damage done to them and just couldn't fight anymore.

Opening the kitchen door I do something I haven't done since I married Sparky I yell at the top of my lungs so it will bounce around the house "Breakfast"

Syco starts belly laughing which brings a smile to my face. Syco isn't a man who laughs a lot. He can be too serious. But since he met Simon he has changed he likes to smile regularly. Watches Simon like a hawk. And takes care of him. He is still strange but it's a good strange. He has too much shit in that head of his.

I look over at my mother who is smiling and shaking her head. "Like mother like daughter"

The door slams open and Sparky enters and grips me around the hips and slams his lips onto mine. Damn I've missed when he does this. It's like he is devouring me one kiss at a time. As soon as it starts he stops kisses me lightly on the forehead and hands me over to Seb. Who looks at me and studies me for a minute then lovingly kisses me. "My Queen" he whispers in my ear which makes me shiver and have the image of him in my bed wrapped in his arms. Smiling I kiss him and say "Love you babe but I'm a kick your ass if you keep anymore shit from me, that also goes for Sparky."

Just as I go to sit down someone batters my front door.

CHAPTER 16

SYCO

I get up and say "I've got it. Will probably be Devil and Princess. Don't touch my food brother or you will pay."

Walking down the hall towards the door I don't hear Princess bitching, which is never a good sign. I decide to peer through the peephole and see Temps and his what I assume to be father.

I shout shit I need to find the keys give me a minute brother and put the top bolt on silently while arming the alarm. I quickly walk back to the kitchen and say "Quick question do you know what Temps dad looks like as he looks similar to your mother Jess same kind of looks." I watch the blood drain from the mothers face and know this might not be good.

"Sofia upstairs now." Marko states. "Jessicka do not mention to him or Temps that we are here. He is the one we need to discuss with you. Do not allow him to sway you. He is the devil in disguise and a fucking asshole to boot."

"Why, why is he here? Surely he can't be that stupid." Jessie is saying aloud and it makes me wonder if she knows the things that have been going on.

"Mum take Simon upstairs keep him quiet as a mouse. And please do not let him come downstairs until these men leave my house." Jessie pleads with her mother. What the fuck?

I have never heard her plead. Something isn't right here. Her mother has a strange look on her face. Yet does as asked. Taking Simon upstairs to play.

Watching Jessie like a hawk I see her shiver and grab a .22 out of the coffee pot on the top shelf and stick it in the waist band of her shorts.

"Let them in Syco. Sparky get your gun and lay it on the table, Seb do the same hands on the guns, show some force. These fuckers think they can just walk up to my house and not have me be pissed is another thing." She seems a lot less upset. That's what I love about my sister she doesn't let a lot of things faze her.

Heading back to the door I pull down the picture of Simon off the wall and put it in the study and shut the door. If she doesn't want these two seeing Simon then they won't.

Unlocking the bolt up top I swing the door open wide with my usual bored expression on my face. "Welcome welcome. We are in the kitchen having breakfast, not sure if Jess made anymore or not."

Both Temps and his father look at me like every other fucker does with barely restrained disgust. When will people learn I'm not actually a psycho, I have been tested. I'm just eccentric.

"About fucking time Sy." Temp gripes out.

Gritting my teeth I count to five in my head, no can't do it "Fuck head its SYCO S.Y.C.O not hard to say. Not fucking Sy. Fucking respect me as your brother then respect the fucking name I was given."

I about turn and they can either follow or fucking kiss my ass. And what's with the fucking suits? Where the fuck is his Cutt?

I march my ass back to the kitchen, slam through the door and then resume my seat. Fucking making me miss my breakfast, pancakes are better warm not cold and soggy.

CHAPTER 17

JESSIE

Looking at the two men, if you could call them men, across from me at my kitchen table, hearing Syco delicately cut his pancakes up and eating them. I look to my Uncle. He is wearing a five piece suit in dark grey with thin white lines vertically spaced about half an inch apart, as much as it probably is a nice suit its hanging off him. Lifting my eyes to his face I see that Syco is right he does look remarkably like my mother, although he has an insincere smile that is blatant on his face, he has deep blue eyes, straight small nose, and blonde hair, his face is more gaunt than filled, it's as though this man is slightly ill yet he isn't, or at least I doubt it.

Whereas this scummy piece of blackmailing shit, Temps who thought he could tell me that I had to give him money for him to keep his mouth shut about me and Sparky getting married without anyone knowing. Oh this little bastard looks healthy as an ox, with his brown hair hazel eyes and square jaw and the added bonus of that lovely scar on his left lower jaw thanks to me and a poker from the BBQ a few years ago. Little prick, literally, thought he could come up to me and tell me that I was his bitch and I was to do as he said although I told his ass to do one.

He learned after the blackmail that he was to stay well the fuck away from me. If he valued his balls.

"What can I do for you both? "

"I'm your uncle, from your mother's side. I am so sorry I couldn't be there for her funeral as well as your fathers. I only heard of his passing a month ago. I understand what you are going through my dear niece. This is my son, your cousin. I do not know if he informed you or not, but I would like a relationship with you, as you must now be running your fathers business interests. As I run my families. We can come to an agreement about you being in my territory."

I stare in awe of his audacity. His territory? He runs my mother's family. So who the fuck have I been talking to then? as it sure as fuck, hasn't been this man. Pretty sure I was informed that when my mother and father married and had me that the families were joined and ran by my father.

That's what I went through all the training and all the fucking books and ledgers for. Not one family but both.

"I'm not sure I fully understand. I run both families interests. You ran like a little bitch. You were never second in command, fuck you weren't even fifth. You weren't in the running and everyone I communicate with in regards to the families businesses have never mentioned you."

He is now starting to turn slightly red in the face "Little girl do not think you run my family. You are insignificant. Just like your mother. She was quick to say that she was the queen of the family, she was murdered in a hotel room on a dreary wet day, wouldn't like that to happen to another member of my family but young lady you are showing that you are too much like your poor dead mother." He says with condemnation.

Chuffing a sarcastic laugh I reply "Little bit too much information you have dear uncle. Would you like to keep talking to me as though I can't and won't take you down the pegs you need? Daring to walk into my fucking house and spew this shit at me is not the way we conduct business. My men will happily lift those guns and shoot you and your fuckhead of a son in the head before you draw your next breath.

Is this the way you want a relationship with the head of the families. Were you sworn in before the priest? Did you take blood oaths? Don't see the scar on that perfectly manicured hand so that would be a no! You ran like a fucking coward and you dare, fucking dare to step to me as though you are the big man. Uncle you are a fucking bug under my fucking shoe. And you have exactly one minute to leave my home before I kill you where you sit and happily finish eating my breakfast. And as for my cousin he knew not to piss me off, for that he will stay and take the punishment from the club."

"You little bitch I'm going to make ..." he starts to spout off and I take my gun and aim it between his eyes.

"Keep running your trap asshole and I will shoot."

He scrapes the chair against my floor in his haste to leave.

"Dad? You can't leave me here." Temp says, showing his fear.

"Son you will learn to leave to live and take your revenge." He says and quickly leaves.

After he slams my door I start to laugh. Takes me a while but Temps is looking at me with a smile on his face as Seb, Sparky and Syco all look baffled and as though I have lost my ever loving mind.

Turning to Temps I shake his hand and say "Well played Temps, you were right the bastard does think he runs the family. And yes he did try and kill my mother. Sadly it was your mother he killed in the hotel room. I checked the death certificate. I am so sorry. If you are still willing even though you paid back the shit you did, then I'm willing to help you find your sister. But you need to tell Devil that you are going into business with me to also run the club that is opening up in a month. And that I want papers drawn up for muscle for hire."

He nods and shakes my hand asking "Any more pancakes?"

"Yeah, but first do you want to meet your aunt?" I reply.

"Fuck yeah"

Shouting for my mother to come down. She arrives in the room and wraps Temps in her arms she has tears running down her face "I am so sorry you lost her. He needs an ass kicking."

"Mother, language!"

"Oh shut up! You got your swearing from me and ass isn't a swear word it's a part of your body." She snarks while sticking her tongue out at me.

Yeah we need to have a long talk I want my mama back.

Getting back to food I finish my food then wait on everyone else to, sending little man for his morning nap and send my mother and uncle Marko for a nap since they have been up all night driving.

"Treasure are you ready to talk?" Sparky asks, and he has been seriously patient.

"Yeah I am but come upstairs so I can get dressed. Syco on watch please, thank you. Seb come on you can help with this shit bubble too." With that said I walk out and head towards the stairs.

CHAPTER 18

SPARKY

I watch her ass sway. There is no other way to describe how her ass moves, she has a sway to that round bubble bum. It's pert and so biteable. It has been a long long time since I bit that ass. And I plan on getting my teeth on it soon.

I can't help but run my hand across her ass as she walks up the stairs in front of me. She stops mid step and turns grabs the hand that felt her ass and does something she has never done, instigated sex. She licks the tip of my finger and then sucks my finger into her mouth, and fucking hums creating a vibration that I swear I feel run the length of my cock.

Seb growls behind me and I'm not sure if he is pissed or horny. But I don't give two shits. I'm fucking horny, I want my wife under me and her pussy surrounding my cock.

"Jessie don't start what you won't finish." I say. She smiles and continues to swirl her tongue around the tip of my finger then she starts to walk backwards towards the top of the stairs. As she hits the top step I can't take any fucking more. I grab her hips and lift her making her wrap her legs around me. As she does she looks back at Seb and raises and eyebrow.

"Ahh fuck it. This was going to happen anyway. Spark get her ass in that bedroom and get her ready for both of us." I can't do anything but nod and grunt.

Fuck I need in her. I've fucking missed her. Her eyes haven't been taken off me since she looked back at Seb. She looks like she is nervous and worried about something but she has nothing to worry about.

She feels the coolness of the back of the door against her as I try and find the fucking handle. Why the fuck do people shut doors. No fucking more doors.

"Down a bit Sparkus. There ya go. Hurry up sexy I need my husband and ol man. I need you to fill me. Fuck me Sparky."

She sounds as though she is as desperate as me. "Treasure just wait I want your pussy riding my face first and you know the fucking rules. My bed my wife my ol lady. You do as you are fucking told." I tell her and bite down gently on her neck which makes her arch her back bringing her pussy to rub against my rock hard cock.

"I don't want to wait Sparky, please it's been too long. I've not had you in years I need you now, no fucking about, now." She growls.

I throw her on the bed where she bounces as I strip myself and watch her watch me hungrily, it's as though I'm a piece of meat and she is starving. She has such a sparkle in her eyes. This is the look she always gave me when I got naked. As though I am her whole fucking world. That look then moves next to me where Seb stands and is also stripping. "First time for a threesome for me be fucking good." He says.

At that he climbs on the bed and runs his hand across her tits and rolls her nipples whispering something in her ear.

"What did you say?" I demand of him.

"I asked if she wanted to have the nipple clamps. She said no."

Chuckling I say "No whispering in my bed, we speak aloud and no one does shit without my say so. I am the boss in this room. Is that understood?"

Both nod their heads while saying yes.

I run my hand along the inside of Treasures right leg. Turning it to run the top part of her leg and lightly touch Sebs leg that lays alongside hers. It's been a fuck of a long time since I had a threesome with another guy, but this will be fucking good. As I get to the spot I want on treasure I lick the last inch of her thigh and swipe hard against her pussy for the first taste, taking her pussy juice onto my tongue I sit up grab onto Sebs arm and make him sit up and I lick his lips letting him have a taste of what our woman tastes like right now.

He hisses in a breath and turns to Treasure and kisses her as I go back to her greedy pussy and my awaiting bounty. Her pussy tastes like the gods fucking nectar to me, there is fuck all like my ol lady's pussy. Swirling my tongue around her clit she seems to fucking levitate off the bed yet I know she has just arched her back with the feel of what I am doing to her. She turns and looks to me begging for something and I'm not a mind reader.

"Baby I need the words it's been too fucking long since I have been able to read you properly and that's my fault. So fucking speak as I'm about to fuck you into the bed."

"I want to suck Sebs cock. Please Sparky please."

Hearing her beg makes me fucking harder. I place my hand on Sebs cock and pump it, feeling every vein in his large cock, slightly smaller than me, he hisses and grabs a firm hold of my cock and starts to slowly pump my already hard as fuck cock. "Baby you want to suck his cock? You have my permission after you lick the length of mine and I want you to take all of Sebs cock into your mouth when I start to fuck you. And if you are a good girl you can watch as I fuck Sebs ass. As long as he shoots his load down your sweet throat while your pussy swallows down my cum."

Seb looks like he is ready for his cock to be sucked and my dick in his ass. Let's see if he can take me.

I flip her onto her knees and tell Seb to kneel at her face and to give her his cock. As I watch her take his length into her mouth and her wrap her lips tightly around his cock, I moan. That's the sexiest fucking thing I've ever seen.

I slowly push my cock into her hot wet pussy feeling her squeeze and contract her pussy as she takes my dick. Hearing a deep hum from her and groaning from Seb I know she is loving me take my pussy back.

I bottom out as she takes my full ten inches. She starts to push against me which makes me start to pump in and out of her with some force loving the squeal every time I hit my cock against her cervix. Starting to roll my finger around her clit she stops sucking Sebs cock to scream. There's the sweet spot, every fucking time she screams at this part. Works every time.

I start fucking her hard and fast and I can feel she is about to cum all over me. I feel the tightness of her and I can see the strain on Sebs face. I know they are both close and I am too but I refuse to finish right now so they can both wait. I feel a hand tickle my balls as they swing and the next thing I know I feel that hand which now I realise is too big to be Treasures grip the base of my cock and pull as I start to vigorously pound into Treasures pussy and all I can feel is the build-up between us and I know I can't fucking stop what is about to happen in the next fucking three minutes "fuck, fuck, fuck. Fuuuccckkkk" I shout as I feel my hot cum spurt out of my cock in waves. I feel like I can't stop. I'm feeling like I can't even hold myself up.

Hearing both of them grunting and screaming their own releases I can't help but smile and then I pull Seb over to me and make him face Treasure as I aim my cock at his tight looking hole. Take a breath I tell him and he does as he does I slowly slide into him and oh my fucking god I feel like this is the tightest hole I have ever been in.

"This won't be long, as you are fucking squeezing the life out my cock I feel like you want this hard. What do you say? Want my cock to fuck you like I fucked her pussy? Do you want my cum up that sweet ass? While I'm fucking you Seb you best do something to keep our lady happy. I want to see smiles on both of those faces today. And to know I fucking did that." I growl into his ear and he is shivering in my hands.

"Fuck me Sparky just fucking fuck me" he growls out.

And fuck him I do. I feel every time he is due to spit out his cum I feel like I can feel his build up in my cock. Fuck I'm about to cum after being in his ass for the whole five minutes I've been pumping in and out of him, watching him finger fuck treasures pussy and suck her tits. She reaches around and I know exactly what she is about to do as ii see that cheeky look, not a minute later I feel her finger slip into my ass and both me and Seb cum fucking hard, me in his ass and Seb all over Treasures tits. I have to mark her also, so I pull out as I am about finished cumming in Sebs ass and cum over her tits with the last spurt and I fall to the bed and kiss her and tell her

"I fucking love you, that has never changed. We will all work through this and become three instead of two. Ok?"

Seb looks up and says "Yeah agreed this is too good to get rid of, plus I am not going anywhere."

Treasure is too busy panting and smiling so she is just nodding her head emphatically.

"We still need to talk though" she says as we all start to fall asleep.

CHAPTER 19

SOFIA

Looking at my grandson who has just went down for a nap I smile. He is so much like his mummy it's unbelievable, he is just too precious. But no doubt by the time he reaches the age of two he will be hell on wheels. If he is anything like his mummy he definitely will be. She was a little shit when she was a baby all the way up to I left.

I wish I could have stayed but if my baby brother hadn't tried to kill me, which ended up being his wife he killed, I would have been there when my daughter was raped, when she gave birth, when she came back to face all this shit. But thanks to him and the plan I couldn't. The plan consisted of making sure Jessicka was safe and that we would watch for a few years to see what my idiot brother would do. Never had I thought he would try to start the family afresh in the states. He didn't even take it from Italy. He started with no one and no books nom ledgers nothing, yet dares to use my family name.

Not on my watch he doesn't, intel told us he was laying low, not that he had set up a whole new family. And how he manages that without his son in toe I don't know.

"He is cute, for a baby boy. He will grow up strong within the family my Queen. How are you after seeing her?" Marko asks as he wraps his arms around me from behind.

I feel safe and steady in his arms yet I know that this is about to get a million times worse and soon.

"He is precious so he is. I feel like a failure, I wasn't there for her, she was violated and I was not there Marko. She went through giving birth and I wasn't there to hold her hand and help her through. Why did we plan this when no one has informed us that my fuckstick of a brother just decided fuck the family but I will use their name.

I have missed out on so much Marko, I hate this. I wasn't there for my husband's last fucking breath. I've not buried him. I never got to say goodbye. Neither did you and he was your best friend. How can you stand there and act like you don't care?"

Grabbing my hair in a vice grip he snarls into my ear "You think I'm not affected? I missed out on everything just like you. Do you not think I want to kill the bastard who took away my best friend and lover. Do you think I don't wish I could have been here to make sure that our girl never needed to go through her ordeal? Fuck you Sofia. I am hurting just as bad if not more than you."

He storms out of the room and down the stairs leaving me in tears as I stand next to Simons crib.

We need to make a plan but first I need to sleep while this little man is. Especially if he is anything like his mummy was. Marko will calm down eventually. I don't chase his ass when he is like this, I leave him to his mood. And a fucking mood it is.

Climbing into the bed I don't even think of getting changed I just need sleep. I curl up on my side and listen to Simon snore. Listening to him breath lulls me to sleep.

What seems like minutes later I feel the bed dip as Marko gets in beside me and pulls me into his arms "I'm sorry for snapping. I love you Sofia but sometimes you just piss me off when you make me sound like a fucking asshole." He kisses my head and promptly falls asleep softly snoring.

CHAPTER 20

TEMPS

I fucking hate my father. That's why I agreed with Jessie with this plan. I take or help take my father out of power, not that he has any, and I become second. I couldn't care less I just want to know my family. My cousins, that sweet little boy Simon. He is my blood. I also wouldn't mind finding out who the fucking rapist bastard is in my club. That was also part of the deal I open a strip club although it is backed by the family it is run and 75% goes to the club. Jessie agreed happily, letting me know all the family would do for the first year is finance it, by then it will run itself.

First things first get in contact with the family in Spain. They need to be informed of what my dear old dad has been up to. As I reach my bike I see a note with a brick holding it down on my seat.

It reads: I hope you are ready to fight on the wrong side my son. As you may be my blood but you will die along with that little whore and her son.

I will kill you all just like I killed her mother and your own. Enjoy your last few days bastard.

Rolling my eyes he is full of hot air, the men he thinks are loyal to him aren't. ok maybe his second in command but that's about it, as much as Smiths is a nasty piece of work he wouldn't fucking dare come against me and the club, women have never been off limits to him sadly that man doesn't care, fuck knows why but he has always been a mystery.

Sending a text to Devil I get on my bike and hightail it to the club, my father won't scare me. There is far more scarier things in this world than him. He just happens to be related to one such bastard. Another bastard that is supposed to be dead but is very much alive, I just need to find him and make him pay for my hurt.

They say things are sent to try you or in my case fucking break you into a million pieces but I digress this particular bastard will see me as his reaper. I will send him to the depths of hell for what he did to me and her.

That's why I will never love, never fall for someone. Never be weak again.

DEV: Understood. Speak soon.

Good he will be making sure my package arrives safely within the next twenty four hours.

The brothers are in for a shock. No one knows well other than Devil. And he only knows because of this lockdown, that will happen within the next twelve hours. Treasure will not be impressed that she is being put on lockdown in the club. But this is needed for safety. There is too much shit at play. Too many players that will come out of the woodwork.

Time to get home and clean my room for my package. Or if you want to be completely accurate my packages.

Turning the key of my bike on I set off towards the clubhouse, not two minutes into my journey I see a cherry red SUV following me and know it's one of my father's men. Watching it for half a mile I know that not only is he following me but he keeps flashing his lights which normally signals for me to pull over. That isn't going to happen, this bastard can follow me to the club and speak to me. I wasn't born yesterday. I won't walk up to a window just to be shot.

Three miles later and I am driving up the road with no sign which takes us a further five miles into the forest where the clubhouse is sat. Yeah I took him the scenic route but that's because if I use the back way two things happen, the brothers know shit may go wrong and the other is if shit does go wrong the towns people won't have a clue and call the cops.

Swerving the potholes I eventually make it to the gates where they swing open and reveal ten brothers with AK-47s in hand and waiting for the prick in the SUV to step out. I still don't know who it is but hopefully it's one of my men.

We watch as the door opens and freshly buffed black shiny shoes and a fancy pair of trousers step out of the car and walk around the door, my jaw is swinging in the wind.

"What the fuck are you wanting me for Smiths? If you wanted to shoot me you had all ten fucking miles to do so. No doubt you know your boss and I aren't in the best of terms."

He looks at me as though I'm an idiot "Boy don't start your peacock shit to me. I know all about it. I'm here to tell you to stay safe while I do what I was tasked and I'm fucking paid for. Now get my sister my brother-in-law my niece and my fucking great nephew safe. Get all four, six including her men, to this club and it on lockdown. And tell my sister Sofia I said hi. Although don't say Smiths say Jason." With that said he gets back into his car and drives around us and out the gates. Leaving me with my jaw still swinging in the wind.

What the fuck just happened? I don't have an uncle, yet according to him I must. I don't remember anyone mentioning a Jason.

"Brother you ok? You haven't moved in five minutes. Packages are on route. Need you to get your ass in motion. Temps time to clean up, and sort this shit out." Devil nudges me to get me moving.

I have never been so fucking confused, how many fucking secrets are being kept in this family. Nodding my head at Devil I start heading to the clubhouse and once I enter those doors it's as though everyone knows we are going into lock down, even the whores know which they need to. They need to go for shopping. As much as we call them whores they aren't, these women take care of the single men and are there to help when we are in the shit. They help take care of the kids and ol ladies they clean they are family. Some are bitches some aren't, some are looking for an ol man others don't care and enjoy the fun they are having.

Natalia walks up and goes to touch me I step away and say "No I have too much going on and after tonight I will no longer be a free man, My wife and kid are coming tomorrow." I turn to walk away and she screams out

"Another fucking one with a wife. What are you so fucking ashamed of her? Is she a mutant? Is that why she isn't here Temps? You happily fucked me yesterday." I didn't even turn around and I heard the slap she received.

"Don't ever talk to a brother like that again. Your ass is on toilets for the next month. And for spewing someone else's business all over the club you are on a fucking brother ban." Princess shouts at her. Which makes her look like she just got slapped by a wet smelly fish. Her mouth opens and closes like one too.

Princess turns to the brothers "Anyone touches her in a sexual way will answer to me. Is that fucking clear. She thinks she can spout her shit in this club she will be brought back down to fucking size. That goes for anyone else. Do not piss me off! Not today" with that said she storms off to the kitchen. Looking over at Devil I see him rearrange his cock in his jeans with a hungry look on his face until

Hawk clears his throat, then that face clears into his usual don't fuck with me look.

"You heard her she is on a ban. Now brothers we are needing church and as soon as I'm back in around an hour we will have it. Everyone get all brothers here now." Devil makes a command and we all whip our phones out and start calling brothers back to the club for church.

CHAPTER 21

JESSIE

Wakening to my door being assaulted. I spring out of bed drag on a pair of trousers and a fresh top and run out the door grabbing my 9mm as I run out the door. I make my way down the stairs and peek through the peephole. Seeing Devil I swing the door open and point the gun at his head. "You bang my door like that again and I will shoot first, then open the fucking door. If you have woke my son up I'm about to kick your ass Devil. President or not."

He just lifts an eyebrow and mutters "Fuck are all women in a bad mood today or something"

Hearing that I snarl out "No I just had a lovely family meeting then had sex with both of my men but to bring me back to earth with a fucking shitty bang you turn up and ruin my happy glow. This better be fucking life threatening Devil."

Huffing out a breath he says "It is go pack once I'm finished and go get your men and mother and father in law or whatever he is called. We have a shit load to discuss and then it's a lockdown. And no bitching as I've just had my ol lady bitch me out and send my kids off with her father, who happily took them off us with a fucking smirk the size of America on his goddamn face so I'm not fucking happy so take the attitude and shove it Treasure I ain't in the mood, unless you can get Princess to take me off her fucking sex ban. That fucking bastard still gets it but oh no not fucking me. I'm protecting her not my fault she was shot. And that's some fucking shit I need to deal with too."

I'm looking at him like he has lost his fucking mind. "Are you finished being a snarky bitch Devil? Ready to pull up those big boy panties? If I get her to lift the ban will you see if your father in law will take Simon away to be safe? My uncle will do everything and anything in his power to take me down. Plus I don't really want Simon in the club, bad enough I will be there."

Frowning at me he nods his head and pulls his phone out dialling a number "Graham can you take one more kid? Jessie's son. Yeah. Ok. See you in half an hour at Jessie's house."

He turns to me and says "Pack him a bag with one pair of pyjamas one outfit and his nappies and wipes so that Graham knows what he needs and also a few bottles of milk. Oh and his Passport. He is being taken on a plane to Scotland. He will be the safest boy along with my daughter and son. Graham will have a fucking army surrounding those kids as soon as Simon leaves this house. There will be nothing to worry about regarding Simon. As much as I fucking hate that bastard, he is one of few I trust with my kids." He's shaking his head and looks through the peephole. "Making sure he isn't near to hear that shit, I would never hear the end of it"

At that I start to laugh. That would be true. Graham can be a complete dickhead when he wants. I signal him to follow me through to the kitchen for a coffee where I see everyone is awake and eating lunch. Picking Simon up out of his highchair I give him loads of kisses and cuddles and say to him "Do you want to go on a plane? Go a trip? Won't be with mummy or daddy?" hearing a menacing growl come from Sparky and him grating out "Daddies. Two of us Treasure, time the boy learned that one." Rolling my eyes I snuggle Simon in and say "Daddies, see daddy and your other daddy sitting next to each other, aren't you special having two daddies? Now you won't be with us but with auntie Princesses daddy. You will go to his house and be spoiled, are you ok with that?" He is too busy nibbling my top to care hopefully when he goes on the plane he will be ok.

I don't want to let him go but I need him safe. I need to make sure that no matter what happens to me that my son is safe and alive.

Sitting down after putting Simon back in his highchair to finish his lunch I am handed a cup of coffee and a sandwich with ham and cheese and cucumber.

I swallow a mouthful off coffee and look at my mother and say "You and I will talk at the clubhouse, we are going on lockdown and I will not give my ahole of an uncle the opportunity to actually kill you this time." Turning to Sparky "Same goes with you and Seb, we will all discuss this after I have sent my son off to grahams. I need to get stuff sorted for him but I need you both to help pack me up. I want all my guns and knives as well as my papers Seb I need them most importantly. He cannot get his frigging hands on them, that is of most urgency he cannot touch those papers. I think they should go with Simon if I am honest. He wouldn't think to look for Simon." At my command they all look at me and nod. Seb knows when I give orders that no matter that I am fucking him he is still my man in this family and he must do as I say.

Sparky knows that this needs to be done and my mother and Uncle Marko, well they know I am the head of the families and I will not stand to be ignored, so they all leave the room leaving me with Devil.

"Anything I can do to help?" he asks

"Nah you have done your part and I cannot thank you enough. But I need to know exactly what is going on Devil."

"After Temps left he was followed back to the club and your uncles second in charge, who turns out to be your uncle. Calls himself Jason. Told Temps to make sure the club had eyes on you all and to make sure you were safe and to be ready whatever the fuck that means."

The kitchen door slams against the wall and standing there is my mother with the look of someone who is about to kill someone. "Jason is alive? Fucking little bastard couldn't have let me know. I've been waiting on him messaging me for the last year. When I see him he is having an ass kicking, fucking ignore his sister will he. This is why I came back. I couldn't stand the fact that after all these fucking years I have missed out on so much. You need to understand that it wasn't by choice I left. If it wasn't for the factor someone was trying to kill me you and your two fathers for my place in the family. I would have stayed and kicked ass, but as soon as it seemed like I had died. You were only going to be in charge of one family, your daddy's. What no one told me was that it didn't matter if I died or not, you would run both families. The deal was struck between me and your daddy's families years ago and was bound by the birth of you. I thought if I left that would have broken the bond, obviously not though, and I don't think Rick will be too happy to hear this, although it would be fucking hilarious to see the look on his face when he finds out."

Well shit. "Wait a minute, so you and daddy never fell in love it was an arranged marriage? For fuck sake. Is anything in my life the truth? Want to add in any more family shit on top of this shit pile? No? Ok them." I turn away and finish my coffee and place my plate and cup in the sink.

"I'm going upstairs to pack Simon up. Then once he leaves we will leave and go to the clubhouse, Devil set up a room for my mother and Marko please. Until I come down every fucker best leave me be." I head out the kitchen door and to Simons bedroom.

CHAPTER 22

SPARKY

Going upstairs and packing our things up has to be the hardest thing I've had to do. I know that sounds stupid but leaving Treasure to deal with all this shit is fucking hard. I just want to take all the crap and deal with it and wrap her in cotton wool. But she is the head of a crime family, well technically two.

How could I never have known about this. She never told me she was a fucking princess. She never told me anything other than her mother was dead. Which ok she even believed that, but still she couldn't have told me she came from a crime family. She knows that my club deals in drugs and guns. Fuck she was with me during a hand off for fuck sake.

I'm now wondering what else she has kept from me. And I still want that fucking DNA test done. I'm going to go take a bit of Simons hair and send that in as he is off to Grahams and fuck knows when he will be home. I need to know if he is mine and her doctors have the dates wrong. Surely it can happen. Highly unlikely though but I want him to be of my blood so he will never need to have it hanging over his head that he is a child from a rape.

"Yo asshole time to get out of here." Devil shouts from downstairs.

I kiss Simon on the head as I get to the front door and whisper "Daddy will see you soon son."

Watching Seb do the same then Simon giving Treasure giant hugs and kisses all over her face. I know this is the right decision so I run my hand through his hair tousling it and pulling a single hair out he doesn't even notice. I tuck it into my hand and wait until Simon has left in Grahams car. Watching him waving makes me feel as though I should be able to protect my son, I'm feeling like a failure yet I know it's the safest place for him is away from what is about to go down.

After he drives out the drive and we can't see the car anymore I go to the kitchen and grab a sandwich bag and lock it with Simons hair in it writing an S on the bag grabbing my hair I tug several hairs and deposit them in another bag and write Sparky on it and pocket both bags and will give them to doc to send for testing immediately. Hopefully within two weeks I will know either way.

Feeling her arms wrap around me she speaks softly "I know you don't know him as well as you want but when he comes home and it is safe for him you will have plenty of time to know him while we raise him. Just keep thinking of that. But right now it's time to get this ball rolling, get to the club. Have church for you and I will have a meeting with my men and women. The club is going to be filled to overflowing so some will need to bunk up."

I run my hands over hers and pull her round for a kiss "Babe why did you never tell me? Did you not trust me? I love you Jess always have and always will. You are my world, ok now I'm adding my boy and Seb to that little world, but you could have told me you were a fucking killer for hire and I would still love you."

She stares at me and says "It was never anything to do with not trusting you. I didn't want it. I didn't want to be in charge of all these people I didn't want you in the danger that being the head of families brings. I still don't. I don't want you, Seb my Simon or anyone I love and care for in harm's way. Look at what is happening right now Sparky. Look I've had to send my son off with another crime boss, ain't that just some shit, I can't protect my kid so I ship him off with another boss. Makes no fucking sense but do you know what? He isn't here to be in immediate harm. If I die he lives and you and Seb will bring him up. My Uncle will try every fucking thing in his arsenal to kill me and I'm going to try my hardest not to let that happen but it's not you and the club he is going against. Its me." I don't know how to reply to her. She is right she has shipped our boy off because, this fucker is after her not us, not Simon, her. And I can't see him stopping until either she is dead or he is. My Pres better have a fucking good plan as I don't have a fucking clue. And I'm not letting her die when I have just got back between her fucking legs.

After she says this she walks out and calls for us all to haul ass and get to the club.

Devil shouts "Asshole clubhouse church now." And I hear his bike growl as he fires her up.

I haul ass with the bag to the car and fling it in the back and haul ass to start my Treasure up. And she purrs just like my ol lady does when I start her up.

"Oi my ol lady better get her ass on the back of this bike or I'm going to smack that ass." Lifting her head from where she was putting things in the car she smiles a naughty smile and saunters over and hitches her leg and climbs on, wrapping her arms securely around my waist I feel her smile as I hand her a helmet with the words "Property of SPARKY" on the back. I had this made for her on the day of our wedding. I've kept it safe all this time in my garage.

"Ready baby?" I ask and she taps my hands twice to let me know she is. And we set off to the club with the wind on my face and my ol lady at my back, as much as things are going to shit, right now I'm fucking at peace and I'm happy.

CHAPTER 23

SEB

As I'm driving behind my lovers, ok I'm fucking confused as to why I was so turned on by Sparky, but, that's for another day. I have my eyes everywhere watching for any shit from Ricky, we know he won't back down and that it will end up being a blood bath. We will try our hardest not to let it come to that, sadly in this life we have no way of knowing if we will be shot through a window or point blank to the back of the head. All I can and will do is protect everyone who needs me to protect them.

My intercom in my ear goes off with Shiva shouting "Boss sniper on the roof adjacent to current location, permission to take down?"

Quickly dialling Temps I ask when he answers "Do you have a shooter on any roofs watching?"

"Negative" he replies to which I press on my intercom on my steering wheel saying to Shiva "Granted maim and retrieve drop off at club. Will see you soon."

All is silent yet I know Shiva has done as I have asked her. She is one of the most deadliest women I have ever met, and she is the best friend to my Queen. Jessie thinks that she is off on a mission for our country, but what she doesn't know is she left a month ago, signed out of duty and is now here ready to take command of Simons protection when he gets back.

Right now everyone is on full protection for Jessie. She doesn't get touched by a fuckin fly unless I say so. As I'm driving I watch as Jessie flinches her head to her left side and I know something has just hurt her. I speed up and close in behind Sparkys bike and as I do I can see a red blotch appear on her arm and I know she has been hit by a bullet, I don't see Sparky being in trouble driving so must only be Jess.

Using my intercom to an open channel. "How the fuck has she managed to be shot? Where is the shooter?"

All my men come back saying Negative on a shooter until both Shiva and Joe come over at the same time with "Shooter down one of ours. Shiva hit but fine, fucking flesh wound."

Jessie is going to be pissed! Not only did she get shot but someone shot Shiva and one of ours turned. This time I'm going to sort it before she knows, that way she is less stressed out.

I watch as Sparkys hand travels along her leg comforting her which means either he felt her flinch or she has signalled to him that she has been shot. Very likely the first one as she refuses to tell anyone what goes on. She's a fucking stubborn little bitch. She still won't tell me who raped her.

I don't think that is something she will just openly share. I tried to get her drunk and ask, never again, I realised that she must have been taught how to handle her drink or she was faking and just drinking water. By the end of the night I was seeing about six of her and I shamelessly passed out as I was trying to fuck her brains out, I didn't even get close to her pussy as I fell off the bed and the last thing I heard was her laughing her fucking ass off as I fell.

Little shithead.

We pull up to the gates of the clubhouse and I see that Temps is standing guard and behind me my guys are pulling up directly behind me.

As we are let in I see a guy who looks to be in his late 30's early 40's with a look of horror on his face as Jessie gets off of Sparkys bike. Before I can shout Sparky over to ask who that was I see Jessie hit the ground hard when Shiva tackles her off of Sparkys bike. If I didn't know the two of them were shot I would be laughing at the way they both go on. But Shiva is like my baby sister and she just side tackled my woman onto her arm. I needn't have worried though, as Jessie swings and connects her right fist in Shiva's face and shouts "Fucking bitch watch my arm" then gets a look at Shiva's right arm and says "Fucking hell just couldn't let me have the limelight, oh fuck no, not Shiva, she has to get the same bullet wound and everything. Bitch."

Shiva and Jessie start rolling on the ground laughing their heads off as though neither of them have a goddamned bullet wound that needs fixing.

"Ahhh babe I've fucking missed you. Where is my sweetie pie nephew?" Shiva asks while pulling Jessie up off the ground with a groan.

"He's away somewhere that isn't around the fucking bullets Shivvy I can't have him here where I know he isn't safe, where he is going he is surrounded by a fucking army navy and the goddamn king. Ok not as much as that but he isn't here and he is safer than he would be here, while we deal with all this shitstorm."

Shiva nods and wraps her in her arms while whispering something no one can hear.

These women will drive me fucking insane before the end of the year. I just fucking know it. It's been about eight months since the two have properly been together and now that Shiva is out it's going to be fucking hell on earth.

"Don't you both think you should get patched up before you pass out from blood loss? Just an idea. Maybe not show your asses to the men and women in an mc. And Jessie please fucking remember you are supposed to be the head of two families can we please act like we weren't raised like fucking weirdos. Do you think that is possible?" I shout across to them which they both send the look of shock and within seconds I know I'm about to get both barrels from the two of them.

"Pardon? I raised that girl so she knows how to act do not attempt to show your own ass Sebastian." Is spoken with laughter at my side as Sofia comes and stands beside me watching the two woman rough house with each other. I swear they are pains in my asses all the women in this family are. They will be the death of us men.

"Fine inside get fixed up and stop Mr hunk over there twisting those panties any further up that tight as fuck ass." Jessie says to Shiva

"Ewww too much info sista. Way too much fucking info. I do not need to know what you do in the bedroom."

I can't help that my eyes trail over to Sparky who is looking at me and smirking like he has a fucking secret. "Fancy giving me a hand here Sparky boy?"

He chuckles and lifts Jessie into his arms, turns towards the main doors and shouts "Deal with the shitstains out here I will deal with little miss attitude here."

At least he gave me the easy job. Won't be long until he comes out here bitching about the two of them.

Stepping away from the car Tonka Truck walks up and says "Fuck head one and two are in separate trucks where do you want them"

"Put them in those out buildings I will be in momentarily" Devil says

As I watch the men being pulled out I shake my head at our guy, Starburst has been with us for three years. What the fuck would make him turn.

None of us would turn we all spoke oaths to protect Jessie and Simon with our fucking lives. He broke that oath. Before I make him take his last breath I want to know why.

He never once shown signs he wasn't happy, he never bitched about anything. So why did he shoot both Jessie and Shiva?

CHAPTER 24

SPARKY

After watching these two play fighting outside all I could do was shake my damn head. At first I was about to hit a woman for the first time in my life until Treasure spoke. Then I couldn't help but laugh at them. At least they weren't screaming which is a fucking godsend. Bad enough I woke up when Simon started screaming Daddy this afternoon but when I felt Treasure flinch and she grunted in pain I was so close to stopping until I saw Seb drive up my ass like the hounds of hell were nipping at my fucking back wheel, was glad I hadn't fully pulled back as he would have been running us over. He needs a lesson on driving behind a fucking bike.

Smacking treasure on the ass I shout above them "How about we go see doc and get you two patched up and feed the masses"

Both women turn to me and give me the death stare or what I would assume is their death stare it just looks like they are frowning while needing to shit.

"Asshole who are you?" Shiva says to me

"Emm that would be my husband and ol man." Treasure replies

"You have two men? How the fuck did that happen and is one bigger than the other, come on bitch tell me all the goss. You can't just say 'that would be my husband and ol man.' Is this a new thing or were you fucking the brains out of Seb while married to this one or did you get really fucking drunk and marry the wrong man. Tell me now. These are the things I need to know. Actually start with have you had both of their cocks in you at the same time and what the fuck does that feel like is it sore, really fucking tight ?? What? Come on Jess."

"Fucking hell take a breath woman. I will tell you when we aren't in a room filled with muscle bound men. Ok?"

She turns and looks at me with a bright red face, what the hell. My ol lady never blushes but she is now and I can feel my trousers getting tighter by the second, fuck she is gorgeous when she blushes. The last time she blushed was the day of our wedding.

WEDDING DAY

I woke to Jessie sitting at the end of the bed that by the feel of she never slept in. She has never slept beside me, we have only ever spoke never touched never kissed nothing. I've never fell in love with this girl and she doesn't even know it, although I've never told her and never will. I want an ol lady. Seeing what some of the brothers have I want that. I want to be able to come home from the club and work and be able to just wrap my arms around a woman and know that she hasn't been touched. I want to come home from a night with the brothers fucking other women and still come home to a waiting breakfast lunch or dinner and not be nagged at.

She knows this is about protection for her also, this way no one can touch her. She's safe from the brothers. If they think she is my steady then they won't touch. Yet I'm still going to be fucking everyone I want. She can't though and if she ever finds out then she can't say a damn word.

This marriage is just paper. "Hey you ready to be hitched? I know it's not anything special but I told you this is just so the brothers know that I am serious. Hands are fucking off you. You will be my ol lady, just without the Cutt." I tell her then I reach out and run my fingers through her hair as I do she moves out of my reach.

She turns to me and she has a blush on her cheeks "Is this really needing to be done. We can't just say that we are in love and decided to get married. What is so wrong with telling people. Actually no don't answer that I'm afraid of the answer, knowing you it will be to do with getting in my panties and having the right to. I love you Sparky I never thought I would fall in love, but here I am on my wedding day, still a virgin and more scared that you will marry me fuck me then walk away."

I'm getting fed up of this fucking moaning, the oh I'm feeling like a little girl. I'm scared of a dick. It's getting fucking old, hopefully when I fuck her she will learn that it's fun and she will be fucking me for the rest of her life.

Wrapping my arms around her I say "Babe there's no need to fear that shit, I Love you, you are my world, I want the house I want the garage I want the dog and I want the kids with you. If that's not enough to show you that I want to be with you then what will be enough. I'm getting fucking sick of having to repeat myself. Now move your ass as we are getting married in five hours and you need to start getting ready."

She laughs and says "It won't take that long it will take me about an hour."

"If you say so babe, now I'm going for a beer at the bar and to play a few games downstairs, behave and I will be up to get you in four hours. Love ya." And I quickly dress in black jeans and a black t-shirt that clings to me.

What I am really doing is going to find that waitress from yesterday and fuck her to relax me. I need a tight wet pussy without the hassle of fucking marrying the bitch.

Four hours later I enter the room to the sounds of Jessie crying. Rolling my eyes to the sky all I can think is what the fuck now? She is just pure drama, do I really want to be with her for life, then I think hey it stops all the club bitches asking if I'm about to make them an ol lady. Fuck that shit those whores have been on all my brothers cocks, I don't want to be saddled with a loose pussy for the rest of my life.

"Jessie what the fuck is wrong now?" I stop dead in my tracks as I see she has photos all over the bed it's a mix of me being with the club whores and a fresh load from today. Fuck.

"You don't love me do you? You don't even care that it's our fucking wedding day. Well you can shove that shit right up your fucking ass, you piece of shit, couldn't even keep it in your pants until we were married, oh of course not, not fucking Sparky. That's like asking for a fucking miracle" she throws the pictures at me and they hit my chest then flutter to the floor and I bend down to pick up the note that was in with these pictures.

MARRIAGE TO THIS MAN WILL DESTROY YOU. BE SMART NOT LIKE YOUR MOTHER. SHE STARTED TO GET SMART AND YOU KNOW WHAT HAPPENED THERE.

MARRY HIM AND END UP LIKE HER

What the fuck does that shit mean? "What the fuck is this? Who sent these?" she doesn't answer me she has walked over and picked up her white dress and throws it in the bin in the corner, tags and all. She steps to the drawers and picks up a little black dress with a red trim along the bottom. The first dress I ever saw her in. She steps into it and zips it up and slips her feet into a pair of black shoes with a red sole. They are sexy as fuck. Sadly I know I ain't getting laid by her anymore. Wedding over thanks to whoever this bastard is.

Tossing her hair over her shoulder she looks at me like I'm built from a steaming pile of shit. "Rule one, don't fuck another in my bed. Rule two don't bring them home, rule three I want three kids, rule four no fucking drama. I don't want to walk into that club and have your whores smirking, the first one to do it and trust me when I say Simon that I will make both you and her pay. Rule five when I walk in or I'm around no fucking anyone. Rule six and this is the big one do not dare step into my business. And finally rule seven don't think you run this marriage I say jump you say yes mistress how muther fucking high. Is this understood?"

My jaw is on the floor and all I can do is nod my head.

"Good, go wash the whore off you. Oh and you see her again I will cut those off understood? Good boy you have twenty fucking minutes dickhead get ready for our wedding. I will meet you at the bar in twenty minutes" and she fucking saunters her ass out of the room leaving me with my jaw dropped and wondering what the fuck just happened.

Twenty minutes later I'm at the bar watching her have no word of a lie nine fucking drinks in front of her and I'm guessing what she has bought in her hand. I know she bought it as there are no men around her but there are about ten waiting to see if she has touched his.

"Ready to be married babe?" I ask aloud, and that's when I see all these men looking crestfallen, isn't that a kick in the balls.

I took that twenty minutes to think through her rules and I am adding a few of my own.

"Right my Treasure a few things, I agree to your rules but number one rule for me is you won't touch another man. Rule two try and give me warning when you come to the club unless you are already with me, if you do not get a reply then understand that I may be busy. I will try and keep fucking other women to once maybe twice a week. I will always be wrapped and I will get regular checks. I agree to the three kids but I want one within two years. Agreed?"

She thinks on it and says "I don't want a Cutt"

"No you will have a property of patch that's non-negotiable so don't even try to get out of that. I've just sent off to have it made. You must wear it when we are at functions and when on the back of my bike, another promise, well two, I promise not to get a whore pregnant, ant never to have another woman on the back of my bike."

She looks like she has just swallowed razors and shakes her head then says to me "Fine agreed" she stands on her tip toes and kisses me on the cheek.

"Good let's get hitched."

Two hours later we were man and wife and she was under me right where she would stay for life.

PRESENT

As much as that day started shitty we kept to the agreement until she left. Or ran. Which I can't blame her for, I still want to know what brother had the balls to touch my wife and ol lady. First things first though patch this pair up then get to church while she has her little meeting. I can't, honestly I still can't take her seriously. I know she is meant to be this big boss but I just can't see it. She still seems like that scared little girl who came into the clubhouse all those years ago.

Walking into docs office I tell him what happened and that both are fine that it's a bullet wound and that they are happy to rough house with each other.

"So what you are trying to tell me is she was shot on the back of your bike and her friend? Was shot when she apprehended the fucker that shot her? Fucking hell what is it with the women of this club and being shot today? First Princess."

"What? Princess was shot?" I interrupt

"Yes asshole now don't interrupt. First Princess and now Jessie and her friend. Fuck sake what happened to women and children being kept out of shit? Fucking cowards." He is shaking his head as he leaves his office and makes way to his sterile room.

Upon entering I see that Jessie has her arms stitched and a bandage on her arm, and she is currently stitching Shiva's arm like this is the most normal thing to do. What the hell?

"Have you done this often Jessie? And who stitched you?" doc asks

"Well, well, well Jessicka you never told me how fucking gorgeous the men are here. Can't believe you held out. He wasn't the one who raped you was he, that would just be a shame if I had to watch you torture and kill him he is just yummier than yummy." Shiva purrs. Poor doc is spluttering out. He really isn't used to women like Shiva. She is in a world of her own, and fucking strange too. But she is friends with my ol lady so I will put up with her.

"Ok ladies enough of that, lady if you want me you will need to wait in line" and fucking winks at her.

She comes back with "Sweetie pie I don't wait. I'm at the front of the queue."

I hear a growling noise and I turn sharply seeing Syco standing at the door. "What's wrong with Mr growls over there?" Shiva asks Treasure just as she finishes putting the bandage on Shiva's arm.

As soon as she jumps down from the table Syco is there pulling her over his shoulder and declares "Fucking hands off brother" well shit.

He looks pissed not horny so something isn't right there. Less fucking drama would be nice.

CHAPTER 25

JESSIE

Watching as my best friend is shipped off on my brothers shoulder, who happens to be her big brute of a cousin. We knew as soon as he heard she was here he would put a brother wide ban on her. Wonder if he will allow anyone to know who she is to him. Shaking my head I berate myself, of fucking course he won't, that would be like making a rock bleed oil. Never going to happen.

"Ready to go babe, go for an hours sleep?

"Sorry babe you have church and I have a meeting to get to. I don't need sleep what I need is to check on my baby and then sort out all this shit. If you could point me in the direction of Devil though that would be awesome. I need a private room actually no what I need is the armoury. That's sound proof isn't it?"

"Follow me babe." He says as he throws his arm around me and looks at me as if I've grown horns and a halo all at once. Did he really think I would put my business where ears could hear. He guides me towards the back rooms and I think surely he isn't going to put me in his room and lock the key thinking poor little me needs to do as the man says?

No he isn't he stops in front of a room that is clearly marked 'Devils office enter at your own risk'

I chuckle softly and say to Sparky "I want that sign"

He huffs as though he doesn't find that shit funny. Well I did.

"Babe I'm pissed you got hurt on my watch. That could have been a million times worse, I'm also fucking pissed off that you won't include me in your own meeting, what I'm ok to be in your bed but not by your side." With that he walks in the door not allowing me to reply. Well fuck that shit

"What the fuck Sparks? Do I get invited to your church? Fuck no I don't how the fuck are you bitching about this? You haven't been sworn into the family. So until that fucking happens your goddamned ass will stay out. If you want sworn in you must have two members of the family vouch for you. And one cannot be me. So you work it fucking out."

"We will discuss this later Jess." He replies. Fuck him.

"Are you both finished with the lovers spat? Yes? Good. What are you wanting?" Devil angrily asks.

Clearing my throat I say "I need the use of your armoury to have a family meeting. I need a room no one will be able to listen in on. And the armoury is sound proof."

"That's fine. But you and I will have a private conversation once I'm finished in church. So stay at the armoury. Message me when you are finished your meeting. Leave so I can speak with Sparky."

I look at Devil as if to say Really?? That's how you are going to speak to the head of two fucking crime families? "Pardon?" I ask

"You can leave Jess."

"Ok let's try this again. Devil, the President of the Canyon Devils MC. Pardon?"

That's when he looks up at me and realises he isn't speaking to Jess wife and ol lady of Sparky but he is speaking to Jessicka Marks of the Spanish crime family Bocecilli.

"If you could possibly go take your meeting so I can discuss something private with my brother here it would be appreciated. We will have a meeting after both of ours have finished to discuss where we will both go from here Jessicka."

"Yes that is fine with me." I reply as I turn out the door. Just as I am shutting the door to his office I hear devil say "Fucking women today!"

I start walking and I can't help but chuckle to myself.

As I am approaching the main room to get my men and women Rumble turns the corner and stops me "Well if it isn't my little whore. Come back for more have we?"

I freeze and just stare at him. This man has been the man in my fucking nightmares.

Rumble was such a good guy in my eyes, was always there when you needed him, always friendly. Such a laugh and so loveable. But that night he wasn't. I thought he was my friend. He never shown signs that he hated me enough to rape me.

I can't move it's like I'm back there again. Back when I can smell him and can't make the smell disappear as one of the worst things in my life happen

NEARLY 2 YEARS EARLIER

I drove to the club with such a happy smile on my face, I messaged Sparky to tell him I would be there today as agreed and that I was nearly there about an hour ago. He hadn't replied but he was the one who told me to come today and that was two days ago. Told me he had a surprise for our anniversary. I laugh because that was four weeks ago. But he tried.

Being let in the gates by a prospect I park opposite the park at the back of the clubhouse. The clubhouse is one giant three story dark grey building that looks more like a stone warehouse dropped in the middle of nowhere on one side and just on the outskirts of town on the other side.

I sat in the car and reapplied my lipstick. I'm not one to wear make-up I would rather just be natural. Also I cannot for the life of me apply make-up so I just leave it unless it's for special occasions. After I put a light pink on my lips I pucker up then get out of the car, I don't bother locking it, I don't see anyone around here stealing my car.

I sort myself and then walk into the club from the backdoor. As I enter the door I hear there's a party going on. Pretty early for a party unless they haven't stopped from last night.

Frowning I try and remember if Sparky said that it was a party night last night or tonight and I can't remember, oh well the worst I'm going to see is a mess and a few men fucking the whores. One thing I know I won't see is Sparky doing that. He promised and it was one of both our rules. No whores when I come to the club.

Just as I round the corner devil turns at the same time and grabs me by the arms before we both collide. "Jess what are you doing here? Thought you and Sparky had an agreement, you don't come unless he invites you."

"Devil he did invite me. Two fucking days ago. He said 'Babe I have a surprise for you at the club come on Thursday after you get your hair cut.' So here I am. Where is he?"

He is looking mighty pissed and shaking his head he just lets me walk passed him. Although as I do I hear "I'm sorry babe"

As I walk into the room after turning left from the doorway I stop dead in my tracks. I feel like my heart has just splintered into a million little shards and I don't think I can piece it back together.

There is my husband fucking a whore on the fucking pool table. Her legs are wrapped around his waist as he power drives his cock in and out of her like a piston.

"That's is babe take my cock. Its fucking yours" he roars out then he obliterates me shouting "Fuck me your better than my ol lady I fucking love you Mel"

That's when I turn and walk calmly out of the clubhouse. I can't go home I feel shaky. I need to get my shit together. I walk around the corner of the building and go to head towards the lake before I take twenty steps from the club I am gripped with an iron grip around my waist and my mouth. I feel a cloth or something being forced into my mouth, trying and failing to bite the fingers that are near my mouth. I feel a hit on my face, its feels like a battering ram and I turn back with fire in my eyes and see for the first time who is hurting me. I have so much shock that I just don't fight anymore.

Rumble? My friend Rumble is doing this? Just as I go to scream he hits me again then he slammed against the wall at the back of the clubhouse.

Slammed so hard I lost consciousness for about three minutes, just enough time to be stripped of my trousers and panties when I came to, I was so shocked and then I realised exactly what was going on.

I fought with everything I had, I scratch I punch I push everything and he still rapes me, he doesn't even stop when bobo walks out the door and a whore drops to her knees and starts to suck him own her throat. I tried screaming that didn't work between the club music and the cloth there was nothing I could do. It feels like it's going on and I start to lose my fight, I just can't fight anymore I know he will kill me after this, I just hope it's sparky that finds me and cleans me up. I don't want anyone seeing me like this.

As he cums in me he grabs my face making me look him in the eyes. He licks my tears and says "He thinks that he can fuck who he wants, like he's the big man. Like he is a fucking God. Well I'm about to show him he ain't all that. You bitch are a message, to more than one person."

He gets off my and stomps on my left leg and then my right arm, breaking both with his black rigger boots. Then he walks away pulling out a smoke and lighting it. The very last thing he said to me was "He is a fucking liar babe you are the better fuck out of you and Mel."

I am too numb to care. I just use my left arm and pull myself up into a sitting position and then proceed to pull myself to the beer barrel and the steps next to it to the cellar.

Once I get up I take my jumper off and tie it around my waist, I won't let anyone see me like this, I will bring shame to the club, to Sparky. I'm going to go home and then get to a hospital out of the way. No one needs to know.

As I pull myself up I hop on my right leg and the pain I am feeling is beyond anything I have ever felt, every up and down it's like a double jar on my leg and arm. But I need to get home before anyone can see me and figure out what happened. It took double the time it would have taken to get home because I was only using one leg to drive the car. That shit isn't easy. I'm just glad I don't drive stick.

Pulling up to my home, I put the car close to the steps of my porch. Taking my time I get into the house and I just can't believe he did this. To me to sparky, actually fuck him he doesn't have anything to do with this. This was me. I was his friend. I need.

I need my fucking daddy. I need a daddy hug. I need him to tell me everything will be ok. That it's not my fault, that I'm not dirty that I'm not a whore to be used.

With that thought I go and get my passport and the money from my safe. It's a couple of thousand. It should get me to Spain. It should get me home to my daddy. To my family. Away from cheating men and rapists.

Away from Sparky. I can't leave him a note. I pick up our wedding photo and I break. I just cry. He said he loved me. He said being his would protect me. Where was he when I was being hurt? Where was his protection when I was being raped by his own fucking brother. That's right fucking Melissa. He tells me to come to the clubhouse for a surprise. Well it's safe to say I am fucking surprised.

When I'm settled in with my dad I will divorce him. Put it as he is a cheating no good lying son of a bitch. Should do the trick.

It takes me a while but I get myself back in the car and I drive two towns over and go to the hospital and tell them I fell down and broke my leg and arm and have scratches and bruises because of the fall. I know they don't believe me but they have to take me at my word.

Once I'm fixed I phone the airport and tell them that I need to fly and that I have a cast on both my leg and my arm. They inform me I can't fly as it has just been casted. Something to do with a long haul flight and risks. So I do the only thing I can think of. I call my daddy. I takes me to phone three times before anyone picks up, and it's my daddy's second in command, or so he says. Once I tell him my name he says to hold the line and he will wake my father up.

After crying for a solid five minutes to my daddy. I can't even speak, he just lets me cry. He knows something is seriously wrong because I am crying so he is allowing me to get it out.

Once I get myself together I explain what is going on and why I can't get a flight out. He says to use my old card and book into a hotel for a few days and that he will send his plane over. But to give it a couple of days as he needs to plan the flight so no one thinks shit is going on over his end. But not to worry that I will be with him soon and that my room is always there for me.

Which sets me off again once I get off the phone.

After booking into a five star hotel under my actual name. I head to my room 517 and I order a burger and fries.

I don't think I can eat it but I need to keep my strength up.

Four days later my father's plane arrives and I am I the air and heading home.

PRESENT

"Cat got your tongue Jessie?"

I curl my lip at him in disgust. I will not allow this man to unnerve me. He doesn't have that fucking power.

Just as I go to pull my gun he speaks "Come now babe surely you want another round. As I said you were better than Mel. But I must admit I was fucking disappointed that you ran to daddy. You did help me do my job though. Felt good to dismember your dear old dad. My knife slid through him like butter with a hot knife. "

"You killed my father? Why? What was all this to do with you. I don't even know you. He certainly didn't." I spit at him

"It wasn't because of anything other than a wage. I didn't know him, but someone did and wanted him gone. Wanted you gone too but I told him I don't kill women, so he turned one of your men. Damn shame he missed because I've been told to rectify the problem since you are now on hard lock down. So stand still and I will be gentle."

I start to laugh then I just can't stop. "So you are trying to tell me you don't kill women but raping them is just fine? Do you know how ass backwards that sounds? You have a mother. Would you allow her to be raped? Didn't fucking think so." As I speak my last word I shoot his hand and he drops his knife, I then take another two shots and shoot his left knee cap and shoot his right shoulder.

"Fucker its less painful than a fucking break." At the first shot I heard and almighty "What the fuck?" by the third I had at least three guns pressing against my skull.

"Ready to be fucked? Nah that's too good for rapist scum like you. My men are going to tie you up and take you to a secure area and then this itch is coming for her own brand of fun. Let's see how loud you can scream fuckhead."

Devil still hasn't took his gun from my head and demands "What the fuck is going on? Why did you shoot my brother."

I sneer at devil and spit on the ground and say "You actually want to call him a brother. You lay claim to him after what he has done to me? No doubt what he has done to other women. Because let me tell you Devil this piece of scum raped me. Outside those very fucking doors, he left me battered and literally fucking broken for a message to both this club and my father. Then dared to murder my father and piss all over him. I will have his fucking head on a pole standing a million miles high for the fucking universe to see. Now I don't give two shits if you pull the trigger because if I don't take him and you shoot and kill me trust me when I say my men and women will destroy you and your club and still do as needed with this shithead. And that's a fucking promise. As I will make that an order to them"

He pushes his gun further into my head and shouts "Fuck" he moves his gun from my head and shoots Rumble in the other shoulder, making Rumble cry out in pain.

"Fucking take the rapist bastard out of my sight. Do as you wish Jessicka but know this you threaten my club again and the peace we have will happily fly off into dust. Don't fuck with the club because you are pissed. We make peace we make an agreement after church and your family meeting."

At that he leaves for church along with Sparky and Syco.

I turn to Matty and say Take that bastard to the shed and hog tie him keep an eye on him. Seb go round up everyone we have a meeting downstairs in the armoury, its down these stairs turn left and its straight in front of you. Shiva come with me I need a fucking drink."

Shiva and I walk in silence towards the bar and from the bar we can hear shouting coming from church. I don't fucking care. I have to take care of my family. And taking care of my family is killing my uncle and taking care of my son. I don't need this club. After that I am very close to just walking out of here and dealing with this myself with my family by my side.

Slamming back a shot of tequila I turn and head to the armoury.

Once I arrive everyone is seated or standing close to the table where I will be standing.

Looking around at all these faces I know what I am about to say will make these people happy.

"We go to war!" at that everyone roars and shouts and stomp s their feet

"My uncle thinks he can try and take over the family business, but here's the problem he is using the family name and isn't doing good things. We aren't the nicest people fuck we kill and maim but we only do that if they hurt us first. Now my uncles second is on our side so we have an in. but this club also wants in on it."

Shiva speaks up saying "Whoa there boss. There was at least ten guns pointed at your head earlier. Why the fuck would we do business with them."

"Shiva I understand where you and probably the rest of you but, one it was my fucking head and we all know that I am the head of this famiglia and if I am to rule then no mother fucking bastard will face anyone but me. Do you really think even though I had a gun pressed into my head that he would have got a shot off? Fuck no. I had my gun against his heart that was why he backed off."

No one says a fucking word. They all know that I won't allow someone to stand in front of me, unless I'm willing to stand in front of them. I may be the boss but I won't say 'you must cover me while I cower in fear' fuck no. I will happily take a bullet for every man and woman in this room and they all know it. That's what family do, they protect.

"Now are we willing to broker peace between this family and the club? This is not a decision I will make alone but we will take a vote. As you all know I am happy with the way we run this family. We vote and if it's not a 75/25 love then we don't do it, but think long and hard as my husband is in the club and princess is here. We can put down roots here instead of being everywhere and nowhere. And we are close enough to our clients and some are far enough away that they won't fucking continue to piss us off, or is that just me with Tobias?"

A couple of chuckles and I start the vote "All in favour I say stay."

Going round the room from my left from Shiva "Stay" from there it was stay, stay, go, stay, stay stay, stay, stay, stay, stay, go, go, stay, stay.

Twenty five minutes later it was a 85/15 split we would broker peace but on our terms. And lay down roots. In which I had the computer guys find me a new house. One that wasn't tainted by that bastard of an uncle of mine.

CHAPTER 26

SPARKY

My heart is still hammering in my chest. I know that Devil didn't know what was going on, fuck none of us did. But when I saw she had shot Rumble my gun automatically lifted thinking this was all a ruse to kill a brother. Certainly not because the bastard was the man who raped my wife.

I still can't get my head around why? Was it vengeance against me or was he just that much of a scum bag?

"Brothers call to order. GIVE IT A FUCKING REST AND SHUT UP!" Everyone shut up and did as they were told.

"Look today has been one for the books, between my wife being shot, my kids being shipped off, Jesses' shit, and now finding out who raped Jess is just a shitty day. But it isn't over. We need all info on her and the family. All info not just the top layer. I want to know where that family shits. We need a vote if we start doing business with them or not. We also need to vote on whether she keeps her station here as she is the head of a family. Sorry sparky but this isn't a decision for you, I did explain this. If the brothers want her out then she is out. We won't make you divorce her and we won't make you stay, but if she is voted out then you would need to make sure that she doesn't know about our comings and goings. We trust you brother no matter what."

Taking a deep breath I shake my head "Do you know I told her that I only married her so I wouldn't be constantly badgered by the whores?"

And for the first time ever I speak the gods honest truth. "The truth is brothers, I married her to tie her family to ours. Originally the deal was made between me and her father. Or technically Dreamcatcher me and her father. Devil your dad brokered this deal to make sure that our interests and our main supplier of drugs and guns was solid. And would remain solid for life. Jessie was never told."

"Once Dreamcatcher was told who she was, he saw me being bitched out by a whore and for the life of me I can't fucking remember who that was. But he always had eyes on Jessie when she worked the bar. He made it his mission to find out who the hell she was. We knew the whores as they came from town, Jessie was a ghost. Jessie Smite didn't exist. Anywhere. So he had a prospect go through her place one night she was working and he got her actual birth name and her daddy's number. Low and behold it's our supplier, who at that point we were having some problems with on our end. A week later her father arrived to broker the deal. We wouldn't kill her if she was to marry me and tie the club and the family together for life, that we would only pay for drugs and guns and not the hassle of getting them here. That's why it is cheaper than Graham. Because we don't pay over what the merchandise is. I don't love my wife and that Cutt isn't worth the leather it's stitched on."

Taking a drag of my smoke I exhale and see Syco with a look I'm scared to say looks like he has just been kicked in the balls.

"So brothers I don't really care what you do, or how you vote. She and her family only mean a deal that was brokered and that is bound by marriage and by that kid. He isn't mine or I don't think he is, but either way he is the product of a brother in the club. So that family no matter what is tied to us."

There is pure silence until I hear "Where is the paper that was signed?"

"Jessie it's in my safe in my room. Go have a look. Your daddy, can do no fucking wrong, daddy sold you to us, or to be more precise sold you and the family to us. Doesn't matter where you go we own you all."

Her face looks like she is finally understanding what I said and why we have rules. I am the best liar in the club. I look over at Devil and he doesn't have a facial expression, although he knew. He has known since about a month before she left.

Let's see how he plays his card.

He taps the table twice with his finger and says "Vote not needed, we own a crime family boys. Let's get drunk and release the prisoners."

"What?" Jessie screams out.

"Bitch, get to your room and do as you are told. Oh and this is for Rumble." At that I shoot her in the shoulder and walk past her out the door.

Getting to the bar Cassie wraps her arms around me and says, I see that you are back on the market. Fancy taking me for a fuck session?

Fuck yes I do. As I take her towards my room I see drips of blood and I hope this bitch wasn't stupid enough to go to my room. Turns out she wasn't.

Where the fuck did she go then?

Five hours later we find out where her and her family went. And the answer to that is in the fucking wind. Along with Princess. Although Princess she went above and fucking beyond there. She left Devil a note.

One which made him become a fucking raging bull through the clubhouse. Fucker landed me in hospital and killed Rumble. A perfect shot through the head dead centre too. I deserved being in the hospital, I just wish what was said in that room wasn't heard by her, or that we stupidly didn't make papers.

CHAPTER 27

SPARKY

IN DEVILS OFFICE AFTER JESSIE LEFT

"What the hell Pres.? When do you talk to women like that?" I ask with astonishment at his behaviour.

"Well I was thinking she wouldn't want to be in here for this brother." He spits at me. Now I can see he is beyond pissed. Just as I'm about to ask what the fuck he is talking about, he slams papers I haven't seen in years in front of me.

I close my eyes and fucking wish I never brokered that deal. I wasn't about to let her be married to just anyone.

In front of me are papers that were written up and executed and signed, creating a bond between the Canyon Devils and the Bococilli family.

I didn't marry her because I wanted to be secure. I did it to secure her to the club meaning that the club would be secured for life with her family. It meant cheaper guns and drugs. Once the Pres at the time, Devils dad Dreamcatcher, caught wind of who Jessie was he had the thought to blackmail her father. Worked a treat, we would marry her off and keep her safe and in return we would only ever pay for drugs and guns not the expense of getting the stuff here. I just can't fucking believe Dreamcatcher made another copy. The original is in my safe in my room.

"Never thought I would have to ask this brother but what the fuck is this shit? Did you fucking buy her? Your marriage isn't even about love. You don't give a shit about her do you? In all this time you fucking knew that she went back to her dad. And didn't give a shit. I always wondered why you were getting away with fucking every woman walking and she wasn't having your balls. What did you do? How the fuck did this happen?"

"Pres at the end of it I did begin to care about what I was doing."

"Stop right fucking there. I can see you don't care. If you did you wouldn't have had a fucking whore in your bed last night. I do walk past your room at night. Tell the fucking truth for once."

I wasn't in my room last night. I was in my apartment. Who the fuck was in my room? I am sitting with a frown on my face and he guesses my thoughts correctly. "You weren't here were you?"

Shaking my head I say "No I wasn't, I was at home packing to move into Jessie's house. Ask Leo he was helping pack. Pres you need to know originally those papers were signed because I was protecting her from being passed around the club. She was going to be a wife, not even mine, on paper only. Your father never gave a shit what brother married her, just that we had the contract. Having a crime family in our midst made us untouchable.

I stepped in to protect what happened to her. I eventually started to have feelings for her, it wasn't until a few months before she ran, but I was beginning to fall in love with her. She was raped and felt like I broke her heart. I was told she walked in as I was flying high on coke and fucking some snatch. I can't even remember that week. But I was planning on taking her away that's what I do remember saying to her then there was a party at the club and I forgot she was coming. Trust me I am kicking my own ass for that shitcake. But that contract is real. We are in partnership with her family. It's completely bound. It states in that if she has a child (by a brother) while married then the family and the club are something her father called blood bound. Means fucking nothing will break it. I fucking wish I could rip that contract into tiny little pieces and set it on fire."

I really fucking do, I know when she finds out it will fucking destroy her and I won't be in her life ever again. Contract or no contract. She will leave and I won't be able to do a damn thing.

I don't deserve to have her in my life but I want her in it. I was honest when I said I was falling for her, she came back and it was like a sledgehammer, all feelings for her hit me all at once. I couldn't look at another woman. Couldn't keep my dick standing to attention without imagining her under me.

"Brother I haven't got a clue what to say or do. What I do know is someone who wasn't that man from her crew shot my wife and shot your, so called, wife. If you care about her and want to do shit properly divorce her and start again. Now as for church and finding the fucker who shot my wife and yours for all intents and purposes, she is legally your wife, but Sparky that shit is null and void. Shit that Dreamcatcher done, all deals and in this case contracts are finished and didn't fucking exist. I don't know if I'm fucking pissed or disgusted Spark I really don't, what I do know is I'm fucking disappointed." He really does look at me like I'm a massive disappointment to him.

I don't fucking blame him, but on the same thought, I think I have to divorce her and start again. I will go and sign those fucking papers and ask her to marry me again. Just make it seem like I want to renew our vows.

Mulling it over I agree with him. "Now how do we find out who fucking shot the wom.." All of a sudden there's a gun shot down the hall, then another and a final one. And a man howling in pain. We shoot out of our chairs and pull our guns and run into see Treasure holding a gun on Rumble and we hear what she said about him raping her but until she drops the gun we hold ours steady.

"Ready to be fucked? Nah that's too good for rapist scum like you. My men are going to tie you up and take you to a secure area and then this bitch is coming for her own brand of fun. Let's see how loud you can scream fuckhead." She screams at him

Devil still hasn't taken his gun from her head and demands "What the fuck is going on? Why did you shoot my brother."

All the while I have my gun pointed at her head steady and ready, I don't want to but I need to show her the club comes first. I feel the press of metal against my head and I know Seb is there, doing his job, protecting his queen.

I watch as she sneers at Devil and spits on the ground and says "You actually want to call him a brother. You lay claim to him after what he has done to me? No doubt what he has done to other women. Because let me tell you Devil this piece of scum raped me. Outside those very fucking doors, he left me battered and literally fucking broken for a message to both this club and my father. Then dared to murder my father and piss all over him. I will have his fucking head on a pole standing a million miles high for the fucking universe to see. Now I don't give two shits if you pull the trigger because if I don't take him and you shoot and kill me trust me when I say my men and women will destroy you and your club and still do as needed with this shithead. And that's a fucking promise. As I will make that an order to them"

He pushes his gun further into her head and shouts "Fuck" he moves his gun from her head and shoots Rumble in the other shoulder, making rumble cry out in pain.

"Fucking take the rapist bastard out of my sight. Do as you wish Jessicka but know this you threaten my club again and the peace we have will happily fly off into dust. Don't fuck with the club because you are pissed. We make peace we make an agreement after church and your family meeting."

With that he follows the brothers as they take Rumble to the holding cell underground. As we walk into the cell I can't help but hum with questions.

With a nod from Devil I ask Rumble. "Why brother? Why rape her then try and kill her and our Princess?"

"I was paid half a mill to kill her. Why wouldn't I, but I never shot Princess. I didn't want to rape Jessie either but it was the only way to get her to her father who I was contracted to kill. I had been searching for eight months with not one fucking hit. So I made her go running to her daddy like the little bitch she is. You should be fucking thanking me brother, I took you away from a bad situation."

A bad situation? What fucking situation falling in love. Being fucking happy, really happy for once in my pathetic fucking life?

"I am not your brother, and if you didn't shoot Princess who did?" I ask

He grunts and tries to move to ease off his shoulder and knee. "I don't know, but I fucking didn't. Maybe it was the fucker who took a shot at your wife? Maybe he has a double contract I don't know. Ask him"

We did but I'm not telling him that. Syco walks in whistling, what sounds like, 'I like big butts' and there is his name sake.

"Pres sorted, didn't know shit other than it wasn't him or anyone in her family. Sorry. Now what's he in for and who shot him?" Syco asks.

"Raped Jessie and has tried to kill her, managed to kill her da." Devil speaks as though he isn't even in the room.

"My turn." Syco goes to step forward,

"No leave him let's make a honey trap. Someone will think that they have got away with it, hide the girls and in church twist the story of the contract. Then we will see who bites." I say an idea taking forming my brain.

"What contract?" which in turn makes us clue Syco in, which in turn makes him kick my ass.

CHAPTER 28

SPARKY

Which brings us to now. Re reading the note Princess left, I wonder if there is anything that will let us know where they have went and if they are actually ok.

I don't doubt it's in Princesses handwriting but surely knowing there was a shooter out there she wouldn't have just fucked off. And certainly not with Treasure. So has treasure taken her, then I automatically dismiss that idea, this is these two I'm thinking about.

"You really need to soundproof your doors. You fucking disgust me and to think the kids have you as a role model. Fuck you DEV I hate you right now. How could you just sit back and allow this to go on in your club. Enjoy the whore in our bed a fucking gain. Come on the fucking new one? Had to have first dibs? You just can't keep it in your pants can you?"

That was her letter but when we got to her room there was no one there. No whore nothing. Makes you wonder if it's a whore in on this, but I doubt it they all learned their lessons when the whore started her shit with Princess, since then no one has stepped out of line.

"Pres. what new whore is she talking about there is three?" I mull over aloud.

"Son of a bitch, I know where she is. She is going to kick my ass!! Fucking idiot. Twelve hours? Yeah I am not getting sex for the next year. Grab your shit and move. She is at her dads house."

What the fuck. Where did he get all that from a whore comment?

"Sparky just hold off on the fucking questions, I will tell you when we get there." With that said we mount our bikes and pull out of the compound like the hounds of hell are nipping us on the asses.

CHAPTER 29

JESSIE

I refuse to think on it anymore. I have an uncle to kill and then it's time to start my life over. I knew in my head that being with Sparky was one of the worst things I could have done.

I walk the length of Princesses dads' hallway of his house, he never left the fucking state but by god was my son safe. Graham was ready for the fucking universe to try and harm him and the kids.

Once Graham opens the door he tells me that he can help. And that we would need to discuss the details of the deal fully but that he agreed to split the are into two sections I take the west side he takes the east side of the country, the only reason I agreed to that was because my clients are all on the west side of the country.

I wouldn't go near Britain he wouldn't go near Spain, but the kicker was if I died during this battle that Simon would be raised by him and have nothing to do with anyone from the club, not even Princess. She kicked up about that until I explained.

Never again would anyone from my family do business with them. They were officially black listed. That contract wasn't worth the paper it's written on. Once I went and retrieved the contract from Sparkys room I knew he was right. I was bought and paid for. But it wasn't iron clad. It stated, if child isn't Sparkys and was the product of an assault on me then the contract would be destroyed. Pretty sure that was an assault.

Contract and obligation gone. Seb wrapped his arms around me and asked if I was ok.

"I'm fine, I knew something wasn't right on my wedding day but I never thought it was that much of a shit storm. Am I that unlovable or am I just a piece of meat Seb? Are you with me out of obligation? Did daddy pay you off too? After we have dealt with this I think I'm going to have a day off. Just a day to myself."

He is looking at me as though I'm a puppy who needs a big hug. "Babe look yes your dad asked me to watch out for you before you arrived and I had, fuck I even kept my distance until you walked in my gym. I fell fucking hard for you and he knew it, so he took me off your protection detail so we could get together. I fucking love you with every inch of my being. You fucking own me. Body and soul. Ok he fucking lied but I haven't. I have never lied to you. And I never fucking will." He grips me tighter as though I'm going to run screaming from him and never return again. As though I'm going to break his heart if I was to leave him.

I love him I do I love Seb with everything in me after the love for my son. As I look over at my Simon sleeping softly, I think about all the shit he will need to go through being the next in line for my job. I will need to teach him so much and I don't think I will be able to allow him to do this, why should he have to do all this shit. The making sure everyone is healthy and whole, make sure our clients are happy if they don't pay hurt, then maim, then finally kill. Do I really want my son to have to do all this?

No I don't but being the first born son he will be obligated to do it.

Kissing his head softly I hear him sigh and smile lightly which makes me smile. This right here is what I'm fighting for. Every step every fall every smile every tear. My son will not live in a world with that horrible piece of shit in it.

"I need to make a few calls. Get in contact with my uncle and tell him I want a meeting. Tell him that I want to draw the line and split the area. Make it sound like I'm scared and weak. Then once he realises I'm not the meek little girl he once knew then I will happily put a goddamned bullet in his fucking brain for daring to try and harm me and mine." I order Seb and he knows the change from his woman to his fucking boss.

I am fucking done having everybody think I'm a pushover, that I can't handle my job, that I'm just a pretty picture sitting on a fucking throne and won't damage a finger nail for this family. No fucking more!

Walking out the room I softly close the door so I don't wake my baby boy. At the end of the hall Princess is standing looking out the window.

She sees me walking towards her and comes towards me and gives me a cuddle. "Thanks for the warning. I can't protect him if he isn't willing to listen. I told him something wasn't right in the club but he just pats me on the head and says I'm such a worrier I'm fucking not. If it wasn't for you we wouldn't have that scum bag under our feet. And I would be in a pine box."

"Princess no tears, I told you I fucking hate tears they suck balls. So suck it up, pull on the big girl panties and lets cause some pain. Yes? Good now give me an hour and I will meet you back here. Go play with your kids."

As she nodded I turned away from her and started walking into the office that Graham has gave me to use for the time being.

As I enter the room that is more like a dream world. From floor to ceiling is books. Don't know what ones as I haven't had a second to look but after this shitfest is done I'm coming back for a looksee.

Smelling the leather in the room, I turn towards the desk and pick up my cell phone and call someone I never wanted to ever call again.

My ex the sniper and killer for hire.

CHAPTER 30

BOBBY

Sitting at the bar with a bottle of Jack Daniel's and a clean glass. I open the bottle and enjoy the smell. I've not fucking done anything since I came back from watching my kid go to his first day of school.

I couldn't not watch from afar. I lost the one woman I cared about because I was a fucking idiot and thought the world owed me what I fucking wanted, and that was to fuck pussy and come home to a cooked meal. That was until the pussy came to my door and told me while my woman was there that she was 2 months along with my kid. A month of non-stop arguing had my woman walking out and telling me I had to be with the mother of my child before she killed the bitch, I didn't believe Cheryl was being a bitch until Jessicka set up a camera in the living room.

Sadly I couldn't stop Jess from leaving as she just left after the fight but she left a long fucking letter explaining what happened and the evidence of why. Let's just say I was pissed enough to nearly kill

Cheryl. I'm not nor will I ever be an easy man, fuck I joined a biker club Canyon Devils out of Alabama to control my temper. Doesn't work as all I can think of even after all these years is my Jessicka. She will always be mine, I just wish she would have stayed.

Just as I pour my first glass of whisky I turn and see Angel sauntering through the club towards me.

It's not normally a good thing when she saunters towards you, but right this minute I'm wallowing in self-pity. So I don't give a shit.

"Hello Bobby before I hand you this, please remember I'm not a messenger, but when I saw your phone constantly going off in the office and then saw who it was on the phone, which by the way nice name for her totally agree, I had to answer and I'm kind of glad I did." Angel says which makes me raise my head at her.

"What the fuck are you talking about? Who called?" I ask her, she hands me a note and my phone. Note says 'Total babe phoned too many ears here problems, need help put phone to ear.'

Putting phone to my ear, not having a clue who the fuck Total babe is I speak into the phone "Hello who is this?"

And my world starts fucking spinning at the right speed and I put the lid back on the bottle. No need for the drink anymore.

"Hi Bobby I need you. I have a problem and I need to worry about my son. He needs a helping hand with the old toy we used to play with. Do you happen to still have it?"

"Long time no hear Babe now yes I still have it, I don't throw much out but I'm pretty sure that wasn't missing the last time, still has all the bells and whistles. Are you wanting to borrow or buy?"

"Buy please."

"Ok babe, do you want me to bring it to you? Or just send it?" let's see if she wants to see me again or if she is taken.

"To be honest I want you to bring it, only if you are able. It would be good to catch up."

Fuck yes! That's the one. She will be mine within the week. With a massive smile on my face I say "Ok Babe I will bring it in two days need to make sure everything is squared away here. Not much to be done. Send me a message with the address details"

"Ok Bobby can't wait to see you. I'm going to head I hear my baby boy getting up." she replies and then holds the line for about thirty seconds which makes me think she may speak. Sadly she breathes and then hangs up.

Time to get my gear together and get on the road.

Just as I stand from my stool Angel puts her hand on my shoulder. "Bobby do you know who that actually is? I need to know so you know what you are walking into."

She is looking at me like I'm a kid who is about to be told there is no more sweets in the world.

Smirking "Angel it is very safe to say I know who Jessicka Bococilli is. I have known her for around seven years. I know her in the sense that I've had her under me that many times I could tell you how many freckles are on her ass cheek. So yes Angel I know exactly who Jessicka is. I may be the only person who does. And she needs me. I'm just waiting on a text and then I will be heading out. I need to tell the pres. I'm off out on a personal errand."

She chuckles and says "You don't need that text. She is at the Florida club."

Just as she says that I receive a text and it definitely is not the Florida clubhouse. It's not even in the same town.

"Sorry Angel she's not at the club."

"What? So then where the fuck is Princess as she said she was with Jessie."

Shaking my head I walk away saying "Fuck knows, but you may want to phone her, as I'm not giving away their co-ordinates."

"What the fuck you mean by co-ordinates?" she screams at me.

I just walk away through the clubhouse then get to the Pres's office and walk in.

He lifts his head from paper work and lifts an eyebrow waiting for me to speak. "Pres I've got a job but I'm worried it's got something to do with one of our clubs in Florida. I'm going to go down and sort it out. Then see if we can come to an agreement with the Bococillis's as Jessicka who is the princess of the family is a friend of mine"

Shaking his head slowly "You need to do better work than that brother. She is now head of the family, Devil is just off the phone to see if we can find her, she heard something about her ol man she shouldn't have. Sparky and Devil were trying to smoke someone out and falsified the original documents which, yeah ok, there is a fair amount of truth, her dad did make a deal for her hand in marriage, but the agreement was she was to fall pregnant with Sparkys kid not the raping bastard Rumbles. So it was null and void, Bococilli family and the Canyon Devils MC will not be in business together, unless you can broker a deal with her. Sparky has just, in the last half an hour, signed the divorce papers. So they will be divorced soon."

I can't help the shock I am in, she was a fucking bargaining chip to Sparky? What an asshole. "Ok Pres I will see if she will play ball, but I can't and won't promise, she means more to me than what you all think." I salute him and go and pack my bag and head to my truck to go see one of the people in this world who owns my heart. And she will be divorced soon.

CHAPTER 31

JESSIE

THREE DAYS LATER

In three days there has been no sign of Devil, Sparky or my fucktard of an uncle. But I have been busy. I officially have a new home. It has eight bedrooms, five bathrooms a giant kitchen two separate toilets and two offices a playroom a massive front room and dining room and one hell of a garden. It's old Victorian and is white. It's gorgeous and I move in after my uncle is destroyed. Which really cannot be quick enough for me.

Just as I hear my boy wake up I see the bedroom door open and hope it's Seb. He went out two days ago looking for information on my uncle. He hasn't replied to me hasn't reached out, and I'm starting to get a little worried.

Standing at the door is Bobby and I can't help but run into his strong arms. I have missed him, I always feel safe in his arms. He is the epiphany of a walking tank. He has added so many new tattoos over the years but he is still massive. If it wasn't for Cheryl and him not believing me on how she really was like, I think I would still be with him. Then I feel shitty about thinking that as I wouldn't have Simon, who is currently making a hell of a racket in his room.

"Damn I've missed you Jessicka, you are a sight for fucking sore eyes." He murmurs in my ear. I slide down off his hips and say

"Give me two minutes until I sort Simon out and bring him through here. Put your stuff down" as he has a duffle bag and a backpack on. My god he is lovely on the eyes.

He catches me staring at his ass as I leave the room to pick up my boy. I hear him chuckle as I reach Simons door, opening it I see someone built standing next to Simons bed. I slowly approach and pull my switchblade out of my pocket.

"Don't bother Treasure. I sent the divorce papers to my lawyer, he says we will be divorced soon. I am sorry that it happened but I'm also not. I lied in church, I do love you. I always will no matter what happens. I just wanted to see Simon, as it turns out he is not mine, and I never knew how much having the idea of a kid made me happy. I am just sorry it wasn't with you. If .. if you want to try this for real it would make my fucking year. But I know that you are hating me and the club. Just let bobby do what he needs to do. Do not interfere, please promise you will stay away, keep Simon safe."

He hasn't turned around. All he has done is pick up Simon and hold him tight, making my heart break. He won't look at me when I clear my throat. I walk over and say "I will think on it all. How did you know I was here?"

He laughs and says "Princess turned her phone on and forgot to turn it off five days ago. So we found her and I knew you were with her. I do love you which is why me and the club will not ask for any help with supplies. We will find someone else." He turns to me and kisses the top of my head and breathes me in, I wish he didn't leave but I know he won't stay unless I ask, and right now I've got an uncle to kill.

ONE WEEK LATER

I woke up like any other day, I woke up at 05:32 got out of bed after a nice stretch to unkink my back.

Walked to the bathroom done my business and then headed to the kitchen checking on Simon to check he was still asleep, which he was. Made my coffee and started making breakfast for myself and Simon.

I heard a thud from the front door and assumed it was the bloody bird that likes to come from the farm and fly into my door every so often, so ignoring the thud I finish making breakfast. I then finish drinking my coffee and without fail just as I'm on my last sip Simon wakes up. Smiling to myself I walk up to Simons room, to pick him up. As I change his bum and brush his three teeth I take him downstairs. I sit his oatmeal down in front of him and start to feed him. After feeding him and sitting him in his walker, he heads to the front door which he does every morning, but as he is there he looks out the side window and starts shouting Da, which makes me frown, does that mean he sees Seb or he wants him?

Walking to him "Say little man do you want Da? He won't be long, promise. Yet as I get to him he is so excited it makes me think Seb is outside. I look the glass window and see Seb sitting against the door. It's way too still outside and I've never known Seb to just sit at a door. Erring on caution I walk to the camera room and check the screen on the front door and my heart stops beating. There is my King slumped against the door with blood coating him, and I know he is dead as his head has been cut off and is sitting on his legs there's a note sitting against his chest and until I have someone who I trust completely with my son I won't open that fucking door. I have to protect my son. And if I open that door not only will he see the only dad he has ever known dead and sliced apart giving him lifelong nightmares but there also could still be a threat. Running to the front door I pick up Simon and bring him to the computer room. This room will survive a bomb blast. Locking us in I phone Bobby.

"Bobby I need you to remove Sebs body from the front porch and then I need you to send Shiva here to stay with Simon. I'm going to kill that bastard myself."

"Babe I am so sorry for your loss. How are you coping?"

"Right now I'm using the rage to cover me, but I will be broken later once I fucking maim and rip this bastard apart for killing and mutilating my King!" I reply and he tells me he will be here in twenty minutes.

I can't stop looking at the front door and surrounding areas of my home. I decide that we will bury Seb here at our home. He deserves to be close to me and his son. I feel tears leaking out and I know I won't be able to hold myself together for very much longer. It's time to take the war to him.

He will not get away with killing the only man who meant the world to me my son is my absolute world I will happily lay my life down so he has the best in his.

I don't know how to tell him his dad is away to heaven. How does someone do that? It's heart breaking that he needs to know and that he was born into this life but I will make sure if he doesn't want to rule the family then he doesn't need to.

"Boo" Simon says as he looks at the screen of the gate.

"Good boy that is boo. Bobby. Mummy's friend. Oh you are a clever and being such a big boy."

I know he doesn't fully understand, but I'm glad he recognises good people.

I put cartoon on the tv and I settle Simon in front of it. Then I watch as Bobby comes to the front door and carefully lift Seb in his arms and carry him to the boat house. I can't watch what happens next or

I will break completely and I can't afford to do that until I kill the son of a bitch!

Shiva comes barrelling up the drive like hell is on her heels. She arrives at the front door as she slams her breaks on her car, she flings her door open and runs to the door and unlocks it with her keys as I unlock the door to the safe room. I watch as she searches every room in the house and makes her way to the safe room, as she enters she looks at me and she knows just by looking that its taking everything in me not to break so instead of giving me a hug she just nods and goes over to Simon.

"Hey big man. Give mummy a kiss and we will go play while mummy goes and does some cleaning. Yeah?" he smiles up at her and lifts his arms and says "Sh Sh" he can't say Shiva but he is too cute to correct.

At his affirmative she lifts him out of his seat and takes him to the play room as I go and get my guns and a few bits and pieces.

Bobby comes round the corner of the house as I am putting my equipment in my car. "Babe we will avenge Seb that I promise. Are you ready for this? You can go back in that house and I will take your uncle out."

I turn to him completely void of any emotions and say "Let's just get this over with I have my king to bury and my son to raise."

An hour later I am pulling up to the house my uncle owns, fuck being sneaky. I'm going in guns fucking blazing. Or that's what it will seem like. I have Bobby in sniper mode, I have ton and Gregor manning the outer area, making sure all guards are taken out. I want no fucking man left alive, but my uncle is fucking mine.

I got in contact with all his clients and explained what was going on. They agreed to move their business dealings to me as I am the rightful head to the family.

I'm not with Sparky but I see the club turned up. in full force which I nod to them and they salute me back. Guess they want rid of this bastard too.

I put my foot firmly on the accelerator and I break through his flimsy gate. Fucker doesn't have any idea how to take care of business, he does it all sneaky and just cares about the green in his hand at the end of the deal. He is sleazy.

I drive up with people shooting at the car but it's bulletproof. I see one man's brain explode as Bobby shoots him, as gruesome as it is, right now it's fucking beautiful. I drive the up all ten steps and crash it through the front doors and jump out shooting the guys in the house as I make my way to the stairs, miraculously I haven't taken a bullet yet, but I also hear the club walk in the house as I reach the top stair. I turn to my left and head towards the bastards' bedroom where recon states that here is where his safe room is, and as I turn the corner to peer into his room I'm shot at, I don't dodge fast enough and there is a bullet graze along my arm.

Fucker, I breathe in and out trying to relax myself and then I step forward and shoot him in between his eyes and his third in command drops like a stone, dead.

Son of a bitch. Room is locked and needs someone's hand print, just as I go to shoot it I hear "let me" and I turn to see Smiths.

"That would be very helpful as I want his head in his lap just like he did to Seb."

Once that door was open, I saw when my uncle realised his fuck up. He realised that not only did his second in command just mutiny but he hasn't a damned weapon in that room or on his person. Well my uncle is about to die in a towel.

Just as I think that he is a moron I pull my gun and just shoot him in the head, I realised in a split second that he isn't worth my rage, he isn't worth me takin time from my son so I would just shoot him kill him and walk the fuck away while shouting to the roof tops he is dead.

Bobby was there to catch me as everything hit me at once, the loss of my King, the loss of Sparky, the one man who I thought had loved me for years, I can't even look over at him and I know he is there, he won't stop looking at me.

I'm a fully broken woman. In such a short time I have lost my father, found out that my marriage was a fucking sham and my king has been murdered. I need to escape for a little while. I'm going to take my son away and just hide, just be a mother for once. My son deserves and needs me to be strong for him.

I whisper to Bobby "I need to get away for a while just me and Simon, are you willing to wait for me? I know I'm asking a lot but Bobby I need you to be here for me when I do eventually break. Sparky is going through his own shit and I just can't cope with that and mine at the same time. Watch him for me please."

He nods and kisses my forehead which seems to be like a red flag to a bull. Sparky comes barrelling over punching Bobby in the jaw which as I'm standing directly in front of Bobby I get hit as well which seems to bring him back to reality as I kick him in the nuts. I know it was an accident but he looks like he is about to break.

"Sparkus I know it was an accident but start controlling your fucking self. Now I'm going home and getting my son. And I'm going on a fucking vacation for a while.

With that I turn and get into my uncles Bentley Flying Spur. I do actually like this car, I may buy myself one. I drive back home and walk directly to Simons room and pack him a bag, then enter my room and pack my bag I head to the Safe room and I freeze.

Sparky is standing directly in front of the safe room door facing me. He won't take his eyes off me.

"Did you really think I would let you just walk away? We need to talk Treasure. And this time I'm going to get shit off my chest.

He takes a cleansing breath and starts "What was said in church wasn't for your ears it was for the one person who was about to kill you. And use me to do it. He set up Rumble to rape you. Or more precise he paid him to. He was working with your uncle to take over the family. Thanks to us that was stopped and he is now dead, I'm sorry to say but it was Bobo who killed Seb. You will never know how sorry I am you lost him, but as much as I am sorry for not getting to him in time, we didn't even know Bobo had him until we saw Bobo drop him at your front door.

Baby yes its true there was a contract between the club and your dad but it was for your protection, your dads knew that your uncle was in the states just not where exactly. So I promised to marry you but he had to promise to help the club, your dad never sold you out. And I did start to fall in love with you. Then you refused to see or even fucking speak to me. I've missed out on my sons life. I want in. I will not allow you to leave here without me. I will leave the club if that's what you fucking want. It will break me and make me not be the man I am but for you and Simon I will do anything you want. Just don't fucking leave me again. I can't survive without you in my life." By the time he is finished I'm in tears and he looks like he wants to cry too but being a man he can't.

In a blubbering mess I just jump into his arms, I can't not have Sparky in my life. I love him. I do but he lied to me. Again. But I can and will forgive him. He has been a constant in my life but I need to tell him something.

"Sparkus you need to know that I am pursuing something with Bobby. If you are still willing we can work this out. Seb was my King, you were my husband. There has to be another king, he takes over after my husband and myself are gone. As much as that sounds so horrible it's the way it is in the family. I love Seb I always will. But I've not grieved him, I'm about to fully break and I don't want you there when I do."

He forces a laugh and says "Fuck that everything you go through I will be right by your fucking side. Now with Bobby he needs to be in agreement, and I guess you realised I couldn't file those papers, I just couldn't bring myself to do it. We are still married and my wife will not go any fucking where without me in tow."

"Fine! Let the club know you are taking a two week vacation with your wife and her son" I say

"MY SON" He shouts

"Sparky fuck off out the way till I get your son then. As he is in that room behind you, fucking move." He moved and I ran in and picked him up giving him a giant hug, I look over at Shiva and she has tears in her eyes. Guess she is an emotional person after all.

CHAPTER 32

SPARKY

After we buried Seb we left for the Cayman isles for a holiday, it was amazing, yet also really fucking shitty. Five days in my Treasure broke and it was horrible to see. She had tears she had rage she had blame she had everything and all I could do was be there for the stages. After a week of her breakdown, it was like she woke up and was back to her normal self. It freaked me out until her mother explained she was like that when she 'died' too so nothing to worry about.

We came back home and discussed everything with Bobby and he happily agreed, although the stipulation was neither he nor I touched during intercourse. Understandable for me. We were all happy. When we got to the club after discussing things with Bobby he had already applied for a transfer while we were away.

I walked in to cheers at being back and asked Devil to come for a chat. To which he disagreed and called church.

"Brother speak." Devil said to me.

"It's not my deal Pres I'm just here to give you my advice." I turn to the doors and let Jessie in.

"Hi boys. I have a deal for you. Now if I walk away the guns and drugs all go with me, now you can buy from Graham if he allows it. Or you can listen to the new deal?"

"We are all ears." Devil states

Licking her lips she starts "We can continue with the deal but one thing won't be happening. If something goes wrong you will be in contact with me directly and not Gregor. Gregor will be dealing with all the clients we have obtained from my uncle, may he be fucked up the ass in hell by a fucking 20 foot pole daily at 3am. Now as you will be dealing direct with me we need to open a club that will be the house for swapping the cash and hiding it in plain sight. Understood? Now Sparky and I are still married so we need to know if you want him out or not. He wants to stay, same with Bobby, we are waiting for his transfer to come through."

She leaves us to discuss all the details and come to a vote.

I won't go into details except to say I'm staying and the vote went 100% in my wife and ol lady's favour. New business and its time to celebrate.

To which my wife takes a drink of beer and promptly throws up into the bin in the bar.

She tells me she is going to my room to lay down and I see Bobby smiling. What the fuck is he smiling for?

He walks up slaps me on the back and says "Someone didn't wrap their shit the last time he fucked her."

It takes a while to click but when it does I run out the bar and jump on the bike and go to the pharmacy and pick up about ten boxes of tests and high-tail it back to the club. As I walk in Bobby follows me up the stairs and into our room. I shake her awake and tell her she needs to do this test or it will be a trip to the doctors for a blood test.

She grumbles but does as I ask her, a minute later we all look at it and I whoop loudly. She is pregnant. She has a smile but you can see she is slightly upset.

"Hey baby what's wrong? Why are you not happy?" I ask as I wrap her in my arms.

"I am, it's just Seb always wanted kids and this one can't be his. This one is yours Sparky. Biologically yours anyway. It's just kind of upsetting that there is nothing left on this earth of Seb."

I can understand that, I can but she knows its ok to think of him but not to let it hurt her so much.

A week later I ask her to come to the club about 2pm to see me.

As she walks in the doors I am waiting for her in the other room, nervous as hell.

I have the priest and every single member of the club and their ol ladies are seated or standing waiting to see her walk towards me. The only problem is she doesn't know that she is marrying me again and she will be getting tied to Bobby today too in front of the whole club.

As she walks in the room we are all in she is standing there with Purple hair and a look of shock, she is wearing a light blue dress which is strappy and falls to her knees. In her hand is a piece of paper and a smile on her face.

She decides to walk towards me and as she gets to my side she whispers "I'm going to kill you for this shit."

"Can you do that after my kid is born and we all get married and tied down again."

She just smiles and nods her head. Trust me the faster we do this the better I need in my wife.

As soon as I'm finished telling my brothers and god that I will love and cherish this woman until death she clears her throat and speaks.

"I love you Simon Marks, I have for a long time. You drive me completely insane when you leave your pee on my toilet seat, when you leave your clothes in front of the basket and refuse to wash a dish. But you are one of the best men I have ever known. I promise to tell you when you are annoying me when I love you and when you are being an ass. But I also promised to apologise when myself, the midwifes and the doctors were wrong. You sent off for a DNA test which came back negative. They sent me a letter two months ago asking if I gave my permission to do the test. Turns out you didn't reply to a letter that dropped through your door you dumb ass. But I replied and said yes to go ahead and do the test. This is me saying sorry I was wrong, but you are Simons dad. Seems he was a small baby even in the womb."

I just can't speak I just stare at her in shock.

"Fucking say something dickhead!" Syco shouts out.

That snaps me out of it. "So Simon is mine? DNA approved?"

"Yes. Simon Marks, Simon Marks Jnr is your DNA approved son. He wasn't early he was right on time."

I gather her up in my arms and hug the fucking shit out of her. One wife two kids and a fucking club full of brothers my life can't get any fucking better.

We begin the party of our wedding and its going great until the door slams open and Shiva shouts for Syco and that its 'her' she has been found. Syco turns towards my ol lady and smiles wide.

"I fucking knew you would little sister." He shouts across the dance floor.

Tipping Treasures head up to me I ask "What the fuck is that all about."

Smiling she says "He has been talking to someone online and he has kind of got a thing for her, yet she wouldn't give any information on who she is and she wouldn't tell him where. Well I had my guys and girls on it and we found her I'm guessing."

We dance until the end of the night when Bobby comes and says its time. Time for her to be his in the eyes of the club.

We walk outside to the table at the lake and there's a bonfire blazing away.

"Brothers we are here to add to this marriage. Bobby will be entering the vows as per club rules state he must be branded by the married brother. Sparky will you step forward and grant him this boon?"

I step forward and hold the brander. Bobby is tied down to the chair and Jessie starts to look like she will be sick. I look at the red glow and quickly place it against his ass. He grunts hard and long I take it off his skin and see he has officially been branded and is officially Jessie's other ol man.

It's archaic but it's a rule that isn't very often used. And strangely no one has changed that rule.

Jessie walks over to him and kisses him hard. "I love you Bobby always. The two of you make me so damned happy but you ever do that shit again and I will be hitting you with a hot fucking poker. This shit is beyond weird."

She starts to walk off when he gets off the chair and steps behind her and smacks her ass "Don't get sassy lady. We have my little princess tomorrow remember."

She smiles and nods and walks off.

"Well brother I'm fucking happy and no doubt you are. I'm ready to take my woman to bed what about you?" I ask him, he nods and grunts "Fuck yeah"

Making our way up to her she shouts don't even bother. No sex until that ass is healed that goes for the two of you.

We look at her like she has lost her damn mind. Until she laughs and runs off towards our room.

The little shit! We start after her and know we will catch her just like we caught her and married her.

SYCO

Turns out the reasons we thought Seb had went missing and turned up in Bobo's arms, being dumped at Jessie's house isn't the reason we thought. Now I need to find out what the fuck is going on!

THE END

THROUGHOUT THIS BOOK THERE IS REFERENCES TO RAPE

IF YOU HAVE EVER WENT THROUGH THIS AND NEED TO TALK TO SOMEONE PLEASE CALL

THE NATIONAL RAPE CRISIS LINE: 0808 802 9999

OR VISIT THEIR WEBSITE

WWW.RAPECRISIS.ORG.UK